Sandra Arnold

is an award-winning writer who lives in New Zealand. She writes novels, short fiction, flash fiction and non-fiction.

She is the author of *The Bones of the Story*, Impspired Books, UK; *The Ash, the Well and the Bluebell*, Mākaro Press, NZ and Aviana Burgas, Bulgaria; *Soul Etchings*, Retreat West Books, UK; *Sing no Sad Songs*, Canterbury University Press, NZ; *Tomorrow's Empire*, Horizon Press, NZ; and *A Distraction of Opposites*, Hazard Press, NZ. Her short fiction has been widely published and anthologised in New Zealand and internationally.

Sandra was a co-founding editor of the New Zealand literary journal *Takahē*. She has judged various literary competitions and has received nominations for The Best Small Fictions, Best Microfictions and The Pushcart Prize.

She held the Robert Lord Cottage Writers Residency in 2020 and the Seresin/Landfall/University of Otago Writers Residency in 2014. She has a PhD in Creative Writing from Central Queensland University, Australia.

Find more at www.sandraarnold.co.nz

Praise for

WHERE THE WIND BLOWS

Humming birds in wild orchids in Brazil, a giant turtle laying her eggs by moonlight on an Omani beach – Sandra Arnold's settings in *Where the Wind Blows* are at once exotic and deeply felt, but equally deeply felt are the inner landscapes of her protagonists as they seek understanding in the wake of loss. These stories, fascinating in their closely-realised outer detail, are also layered in their examination of what it means to be family, both the immediate family and the wider human family.

James Norcliffe,
author of *Letter to Oumuamua*
and winner 2022 NZ Prime Minister's Award
for Literary Achievement

WHERE THE THE WIND *BLOWS*

SANDRA ARNOLD

TRUTH SERUM PRESS

Truth Serum Press
32 Meredith Street
Sefton Park SA 5083
Australia

Email: truthserumpress@live.com.au
Website: truthserumpress.net
Catalogue: truthserumpress.net/catalogue

Cover design copyright © Matt Potter
Cover image copyright © Taru Kurenmaa
Author photograph copyright © Chris Arnold

Also available as an ePub eBook
ISBN: 978-1-923000-26-1
Also available as a Kindle eBook
ISBN: 978-1-923000-30-8

Truth Serum Press is a member of the
Bequem Publishing collective
bequempublishing.com

For Chris

Contents

Brazil 1995

1   Just an old grey Volkswagen

11   The man in the moon

21   The season for burning

36   The colour of sunshine

46   Pablo's hair

55   The night of the goddess

New Zealand 2002 – 2003

67   The bough breaks

76   Grit

78   Time to leave

82   The quick and the dead

89   The skin that separates water and air

101   When the wind died

Oman 2003 – 2004

117   Connecting

142   Bridging the gap

146   I'll get back to you

155   Dawn trek in the Wahiba Desert

158   Team-building

161   Kassidy's roof

179   The stone

188   The desert wind and the
           tinkling of the camel's bell

198   Disconnecting

Brazil 2004

209   Shadows

New Zealand 2004 – 2007

219   A different road

222   New beginnings

Brazil

1995

Just an old grey Volkswagen

"My father has a little store in Amazonas," Bernado said. "He sells bread, *guarana*, rice and beans. When I phoned him to tell him I'd passed my exams to go to university he had a party to celebrate." He grinned. "So now I can work, I can study and I have already bought a small piece of land." He sprang off the sofa and over to the window. We followed the direction of his outstretched arm over the spire of the little blue church that looked so much like a music box that if I could have lifted off the roof, I felt sure I would see the priest and congregation spinning in small circles beneath. Bernado pointed over the clogged streets of the city, past the high-rise office blocks and apartment buildings, to the shacks of the outer suburbs. He breathed deeply. "I have put a deposit on my land and I pay it off every month. In five years it will be mine and on my land I will build my house. Then, *dona* Alexa, I will buy a nice car and a computer."

"But what will you do for money, now you've lost your job?" I asked.

He shrugged. "I've started teaching English at a high school near where I live. It's not as much as I was getting here, as a receptionist, because I have just three times a week teaching, but they might give me some more classes soon. And I sell popcorns in the street."

Beth looked at him. "I think it really sucks that they sacked you. None of the other receptionists can even speak English. When they see us coming it's like, hey, we're all suddenly very busy!"

"Well, soon you will be able to speak Portuguese," he said. "Then you won't have those problems no more. But, speaking of English, I would like to invite you to my school to meet my students. I've told them all about you and they want to practise their English with you. They are very excited that there are some foreigners here in Uberlândia. Will you come to meet them? I could pick you up in my car at 6.30."

The sky turned from black to pearly grey as we waited on the pink marble wall outside the apartment building. Aromas of fresh bread drifted on the warm air. Further down the street the man from the bread shop emerged to begin his daily ritual of hosing down the pavement. He directed a jet of water onto piles of plastic cups and cigarette butts and washed them away from his patch to the gutter in front of the shop next door.

A sound like thousands of metal chips grinding inside a giant concrete mixer heralded the first buses arriving at the square to collect the early commuters. Three car alarms began wailing.

Beth, yawning pointedly, looked at her watch for the umpteenth time. "It's quarter to seven. I could've been in bed all this time. He must have forgotten. I'm outta here!"

I was about to follow her. I didn't want to be down there when the advertising trucks began their rounds. With loudspeakers bigger than the rooms in our apartment those trucks brought a new dimension to the meaning of noise. There was no escape, but at least on the sixteenth floor we could close the windows.

Before Beth reached the swing doors I saw an old grey Volkswagen chug up to the building. I didn't know whether to feel relieved or sorry.

Bernado stuck his head out the window. "Sorry I'm late. I had a small problem starting my car!"

I had great difficulty controlling my smile at Beth's expression as she trudged back, but she erased the scowl from her face as she reached the car. Bernado leapt out and opened the door to let us in. I settled into my seat. Immediately the back fell off. I gasped. Beth stifled a giggle. Bernado clicked his tongue in exasperation.

"Sorry about that. It happens sometimes. But don't worry. I have a piece of wood I will fix it with before the return journey."

I looked around for the seat belt and out of the corner of my eye saw Beth in the back seat, convulsing with silent laughter. I was grateful for her attempt at self-control, but there was no seat belt and as we drove over the first speed hump I lurched forward and grabbed the dashboard. It gave way under my hands then I saw that it was held together with several layers of sticky tape.

"Don't worry about that," Bernado reassured. "I'm driving very slowly so the dashboard will not fall apart. You know the roads here are so bad that it makes the dashboard to deform if I drive too fast. Also my steering wheel will come out because it is loose. But don't worry," he added, seeing my expression, "I am holding it in very carefully. I am going to spend some time fixing a few things about my car this weekend."

We cruised up to a red traffic light and the car started rolling backwards.

I held onto the sides of my seat. "Brake, Bernado?"

He nodded cheerfully. "I'm going to fix the brakes this weekend."

A motorbike carrying two adults and three children overtook us and sped straight through the lights. One of the children was carrying a goose under his arm. Three oncoming cars swerved and honked their horns. One of the swerving cars had a wardrobe on its roof. The driver and front passenger each had an arm out of the window holding onto the side of the wardrobe. Another man was standing on the back bumper also hanging onto the wardrobe. They waved and shouted a greeting to the family on the motorbike who waved back.

"My God! They could have been killed!"

"Yes," Bernado agreed. "But if they are all killed together that's better. It means there is nobody left to cry."

I looked at him to see if he was joking, but he wasn't smiling. His car had now rolled into the bus behind. He glanced in his rearview mirror, but as there was a large crack right across it, I doubted he could see anything.

"Unfortunately, there are some very bad drivers in this city," he said. "Most of them doesn't have a licence." He smiled shyly, "I got my license in the Amazon. Are you surprised to hear that?"

"Well …"

"Ha! You thought there were no roads in the Amazon. Right?" His smile grew wider.

The lights changed to green and his car started to crawl forward. "Well, you might be even more surprised to know that I bought this car in the Amazon. When I came to live in Uberlândia I paid for my car to be brought here by truck."

The bus driver was honking impatiently and cars roared around us. One mounted the pavement to squeeze by and the pedestrians flattened themselves against the wall to allow it to pass.

Bernado swerved around the cars. "No problem," he said, as I dug my fingers into the dashboard. It crunched alarmingly under the sticky tape. "This is a one-way street. It's a good short-cut."

"I really think we should get back onto the proper road."

"We're nearly there," he said. "Just around the corner is the school."

We pulled up in front of a long, low building behind a peeling white wall covered in graffiti. I looked for a handle on the door so I could open it, but there wasn't one.

"There is a secret to getting out of my car," Bernado said, leaning across and pushing down the window. "Now, lean out the window and open the door from the outside."

I staggered out and Bernado called from the car. "I'll be with you soon. I'm just locking my car to stop thieves stealing it. I invented this special lock myself."

Beth joined me on the pavement. She didn't look at me, but from the way her shoulders were shaking I knew she was on the point of bursting.

Bernado undid a piece of wire that attached the rusty gate to the gatepost and led us into the small concrete schoolyard. Groups of teenagers were standing under an iron roof that extended from the main building. It was their only shelter from the already blisteringly hot sun. They smiled and greeted us and stared at Beth.

"This is a high school?" she whispered, incredulous.

Two middle-aged women in jeans and T-shirts were busy arranging coffee cups and biscuits in the staff room. Bernado introduced them as the principal and deputy principal. They shook hands and welcomed us. While we sat on a worn leather sofa drinking thick, black coffee, they asked Beth, in English, to tell them about her high school in New Zealand. Even her reluctant, lukewarm description was enough to make their eyes widen.

"You are so lucky," the principal said. "But I suppose you already know that." She gestured around the dingy room. "I know what you must be thinking. But this year I asked the government for money to upgrade all the buildings. We received only twenty five percent of what we asked for, so what can we do?"

She asked us what we thought of Uberlândia.

"The people are lovely," I said.

"And the city? Did you know that uber means cow's udder?"

"Good name," murmured Beth.

To my relief the principal didn't pick up the tone and looked pleased. "Yes, indeed. It's another way of saying this is a land of milk and honey. We're very proud of our city. Apart from the capital it's the most developed city in Minas Gerais. Some people even say that in a few years it will be the capital instead of Belo Horizonte."

After coffee, Bernado led us along the corridor into his classroom. The noise, like several hundred seagulls screaming on a rock, subsided as we entered, and about forty teenagers found their way back to their seats, beaming at us. They'd practised their questions in English:

"What is the population of New Zealand?"

"What is the weather like?"

"Do you like Brazilian food?"

"Are there only white people in New Zealand?"

As we answered, they climbed onto their desks to listen. Eventually they were all sitting on the front row of desks. One boy said to Beth, "You are very beautiful. Do you have a boyfriend?" The class erupted in delighted laughter.

Bernado smiled. "I don't get too strict with them. If I got strict I'm afraid they might not come to school, so I try to make it fun for them."

At the end of our question-and-answer session the children swarmed around us, wanting our autographs, asking us to return. The boy who'd asked Beth about boyfriends was sitting at the back of the class, drawing. He came forward and presented his picture to her as a memento of the day. It was a pencil sketch of Donald Duck. She smiled and thanked him in Portuguese. It was the first time I'd heard her speak Portuguese despite the fact we'd been taking lessons since we arrived in the city a month ago. The children were delighted and wanted her to say more, but Bernado managed to lead us out the door by promising the class we would return.

"What did you think of them, Beth?" he asked, outside.

"How can they be that cheerful in such a dump?"

"They are happy because they have a school to go to," Bernado said. "Many of our children doesn't go to school."

The return journey was not quite as hair-raising because, true to his word, Bernado had fixed the back of the front passenger seat with a piece of wood. I was careful, however, not to lean on it too heavily.

He entered the apartment building with us because he wanted to stay and chat to his friends at the reception desk. We said goodbye and hurried into the lift. Beth managed to control herself long enough for the lift door to close then she sank to the floor, tears splashing down her face. Still shocked that I had let her stay in that car, I couldn't breathe. The lift stopped at the next floor and a man stepped in, looked at Beth and hurriedly stepped out at the next floor. I was enormously embarrassed. The lift stopped at our floor. Beth stumbled along the corridor and into our apartment. She threw herself spread-eagled on her bed and screamed with laughter.

Twenty minutes later we were sitting on the little balcony drinking pineapple juice.

"Oh Mum, you should have seen your face when the back of the seat fell off, I thought I was going to die!"

"I can't believe that car!" I said. "I can't believe I let you stay in it. Why didn't we just get out?"

"How come a car like that is even allowed on the road?" Beth said.

"He's a sweet man," I said, "but if he ever offers to take us anywhere again we'll have to think of a polite excuse to refuse."

The doorbell rang. When I opened the door, Bernado stood there with a shy smile on his face. "I want to give you a present for coming to my school today."

"No, that isn't necessary, Bernado," I protested, a blush of shame creeping up my neck.

"But anyway, I want you to have it," he said and produced a package from behind his back and handed it to Beth. "It's for you both."

She untied the gold ribbon and unwrapped the yellow tissue paper. Inside was a framed photograph of a truck laden with brand new cars. In the middle of them was the old Volkswagen.

"My car," Bernado said. "In the truck that brought it from the Amazon. It is my fourth car. And my best. The truck driver took this photograph for me. Now I want you to have my photograph. So you will always remember this day."

The man in the moon

"So what was it like the first time you did it?" I heard Beth say.

The sand was burning my feet, so I hid my shock by hobbling over to my chair and rubbing my blistered toes. Beth and a girl she'd met on the beach, Gabriella, were gazing at the young waiter with shining eyes.

"No problems at the time. But that night I had fried chicken for dinner. I peeled off the skin and ..."

The girls leaned forward.

"I had to run to the bathroom. I've never been able to eat fried chicken since."

Beth shuddered. "Gross!"

Gabriella paled beneath her tan.

I held my breath, bewildered.

The waiter added, "We are never told the person's name, or how they died. But every time I pick up the knife I hurt in my heart and I say, *I'm sorry. I don't know who you are, but I hope you had a good life.*"

"On your first day!" gasped Beth.

The waiter shrugged. "You can't study medicine if you're squeamish."

My breath escaped. Beth glanced at me. I gabbled, "I hope you don't mind orange juice again." I can choose *mamão, abacaxi, acerola* and *pêssego*, but after six weeks I still haven't got my tongue around the Portuguese pronunciation.

"*Abacaxi?*" the waiter offered.

"No! Let her ask herself. Go on, Mum, I dare you!"

Gabriella reassured me, "When we went to the States last year my father made me do all the talking because I was the only one in the family who spoke English." She was the same age as Beth, holidaying in Porto Seguro with her family to escape Carnival frenzy in Rio.

The manager's young son stood by expectantly. The girls were looking at me, amused.

"*Um suco de abacaxi, por favor,*" I tried.

"*Com açucar?*" said the boy.

"*Não, sem açucar.*" I was childishly pleased with my success.

Gabriella hugged me.

Beth conceded, "Not bad!"

The waiter grinned. "Brazilians will never laugh at you for trying."

He had little crinkly lines around his large brown eyes. They deepened as he laughed.

"My uncle spent two years in the USA. He had a good job and made a lot of money, but he was very lonely, so he came back home. 'Those cold-hearted people,' he told me, 'they don't care about you.' Is it the same in New Zealand?"

Before I could answer, Beth grabbed him and Gabriella and hauled them off to join the *lamba-aerobics* session led by two Bahian youths with bodies of rubber. I watched her swinging her hips in her new red *tanga*. The music blasted out of the loudspeakers at brain-shattering volume while a small boy hosed down the sweating dancers. A couple of large middle-aged women in luminous pink and turquoise *tangas* joined the group. I looked at them longingly, wondering if I would dare. No. I wouldn't. I found an empty sun-lounger to stretch out on instead.

Rob came back from his swim, towelling himself as he strode over the sand. He caught sight of Beth dancing. He stopped towelling and touched the back of my neck then spied another hawker with an armful of hammocks advancing towards us. He groaned, "I'm off. Coming?"

I shook my head and covered my face with a towel so I could ignore the hawker's banter, but I was so unaccustomed to lying still that I couldn't stay long on the sun-lounger. I threw on my wrap, left the beach, and wandered over to the marketplace.

Music throbbed in the mango-scented air. A space cleared in the crowd and I saw a little string puppet dancing the samba on the cobblestones. Children, teenagers, middle-aged and old people began to imitate the puppet, swaying their own hips and swinging their arms above their heads. The unexpectedness of it all made me laugh out loud.

I bought a coconut from a young woman at a stall. She sliced the top off with a heavy flat-bladed knife, poked a hole in and stuck a straw through. A tiny girl about two years old sat beside the stall. She was dressed in pink with a pink bow in her curly, black hair. I smiled at her, but she sucked harder on her dummy. I sat on the grass next to the stall, sipping the coconut juice, watching people dancing in the streets and milling in and out of the little pink and yellow shops. I turned to see the girl stand and wander a few steps away from the stall. Her mother paused in the act of chopping off the top of a coconut and shouted at her, pointing to the spot she had just left. The child ignored the command. The woman raised her arm and whacked her over the leg with the flat of the knife. The child fell over, spread-eagled on the concrete. I jumped up and reached out my arms, but she scrambled on her hands and knees back to the place she had been sitting and began to howl. I gaped at the woman. She looked embarrassed for a minute, then tilted her chin and stared at me.

I turned away, telling myself it wasn't my business, and almost stumbled over a young artist sketching the portrait of a teenage girl. I found a space on a wall where I could sit and brush away my tears unobserved. My heart was pounding. I tried to concentrate on the artist. The girl he was drawing was very pretty, but from her anxious glances at the easel I saw she was eager to know how she was being portrayed to the little crowd which had gathered to watch.

"Your father's contract in Brazil has been confirmed. We'll get there in time to celebrate Carnival in Porto Seguro. Isn't that great?"

"I'm not going. The horse show's coming up. I want to stay at home with Olivia and Sam."

"They're at university. They won't have time to keep an eye on you."

Beth didn't look up from her pile of horse magazines. "So you expect me to give up my LIFE to live in a third-world DUMP where nobody even speaks ENGLISH? No way. I'm not going."

We'd arrived in Uberlândia in the rainy season. Rob spent every day at work. Beth stayed in her bedroom with the door shut, the boxes of Correspondence School material unopened on the floor. I sat on the balcony of our sixteenth-floor apartment watching the vultures circling in the khaki sky. Sometimes they landed on rooftops, stretching their scrawny necks and ragged black wings. One morning I opened the curtains to see two sitting on the rail, looking at me with hard little eyes.

The sun rose higher in the sky. Balls of light bounced off the sea. People danced in the street. A young couple sat down beside me. The artist finished his picture and began another painting.

"*Senhora, tudo bem?*" The young couple peered at me anxiously.

Startled, I looked back at them, unable to get them into focus, then realised tears were streaming down my face. The girl opened her bag and took out a packet of tissues and handed them to me. Like a child I took one to wipe my eyes. "*Obrigada,*" I murmured and stood up to go because she was looking so concerned.

I walked past the coconut stall again and looked for the baby, but she wasn't there. To my relief her mother was too busy counting change to notice me.

By the time I arrived at the beach my skin was on fire. I rummaged in my bag and found the sunblock. Beth threw herself on the sun-lounger beside me panting and sweating.

"That was soooo cool!"

She had that rare combination of dark blonde hair and deep gold skin. She was as smooth as an egg. I needed to touch her, so I rubbed sunblock on her neck.

Gabriella was saying that in Rio the biggest problem for rich people was the threat of kidnap. "They're afraid to leave their houses. Their homes are their prisons."

The waiter replied that two years ago his uncle was killed in Rio. "He stopped to ask directions. In some parts of the city it's too dangerous even to stop at traffic lights. They shot him. My grandfather was so worried, he had an accident on the way to the hospital. He too was in intensive care. My uncle died next day. For a week we had to lie to my grandfather. Even to my uncle's wife, because she was pregnant with their first child." He looked at his hands. "It was a terrible time for my family. It was then I decided to be a doctor."

He told us he grew up on his father's farm. When he'd decided to go to university he wasn't able to pass his exams because he'd gone to a state school. "The government does not give those schools enough money, so there are not enough facilities. The teachers are poorly paid, so they are always striking. I had to go to a private school for a year to prepare for my exams. My grandmother paid for me to do that. If it hadn't been for my grandmother I would have ended up studying veterinary science instead of medicine."

"Ended up?" laughed Beth. "In New Zealand it's harder to get into vet school than med school!"

The waiter's eyes widened. "You mean animals are more important than people in your country?"

Beth glared at him. Gabriella quickly changed the topic. "Your parents must have been very happy when you passed your exams."

The waiter shook his head. "My father wanted me to stay on the farm. When my results came out I was so happy I cried. But my father still won't speak to me. So I work my vacations here, to earn money for my books."

"No one celebrated when you passed your exams?" I asked.

"Only my grandmother. She fell down on her knees and thanked God. She's a very religious woman." He smiled. "Are people in New Zealand religious?"

"Some."

"And you, *Senhora?*"

"No."

"Oh? In Brazil we have many religions." He pointed to a group of women in voluminous white lacy dresses selling coconut, ginger, cinnamon and honey cakes by the side of the beach. "Their religion is *Macumba,* a kind of black magic. It was brought here by the African slaves and when their Portuguese owners forbade them to practise it, they disguised their gods as Catholic Saints. That's why *Iemanja,* their Goddess of the Sea, looks like the Virgin Mary."

Beth wanted to know more. Her eyes shone with curiosity.

The manager approached, saw us watching the women and said something to the waiter and Gabriela in Portuguese. Whatever it was it was obviously very funny as the three of them burst out laughing. Beth watched them enjoying a joke she couldn't understand. She rummaged for something in her bag, pretending not to care.

I stepped out of the shower and stood in front of the mirror looking critically at my body. I had just scrubbed it from neck to toe with a loofah. I passed my hands over my skin and noted how soft it felt. I smoothed the worry lines away from my eyes, ran my fingers through my sun-bleached hair. Through the mirror I saw Rob lying on the bed slicing pieces of mango.

Beth swung in the hammock. "What's the Portuguese word for joke?"

Rob tossed her the dictionary.

I sat on the bed squirting cream onto my legs and arms. The sun had seeped into my bones.

Rob took the bottle from me, poured cream into his hand and rubbed it in my back. His hand was warm. I leaned into it. He popped a piece of mango into my mouth.

Beth closed the dictionary, rolled out of the hammock and headed for the shower. "All Gabriella's family are going to the beach party tonight. Can we go?"

Coconut palms lined the road to the beach. A man sat at the top of a tree, hacking off coconuts with a long-curved knife. Behind him the clouds were dark smudges on an opal sky. I crossed the road to the beach. A few people sat at tables inside the *cabana,* ordering their dinner. The waiter saw me pass by and waved. I thought he would have already left for the party. The beach umbrellas were folded and stacked neatly on the sand. The seats were all empty. I found one near the edge of the sea. Music from the *Trio Eletrica* drifted down the beach. The colours faded from the sky and the sea turned milky. A sliver of red appeared on the line where the sky met the sea. The moon rose, silvering the water with jagged light.

"*A lua,* she is very beautiful. I like to watch her rise every night." The waiter padded over to where I was sitting. "If I was an artist I would paint it."

"Me too," I said, and realised I didn't even know his name.

"Leonardo," he answered, before I could form the question.

The sand squeezing between my bare toes was warm. The music vibrated in my bones. A young man danced with a sleeping baby on his shoulder. Behind him a little girl danced with an old man. Gabriella's family danced in the sea. The crew on a fishing boat clapped their hands to the beat of the band. Rob pulled me close.

"And they danced by the light of the moon, the moon, they danced by the light of the moon," Beth crooned.

"All except us," said Leonardo, reaching for her hands.

"I don't know how to," she said, suddenly awkward.

"It's very easy. I'll teach you."

The moon hung over the sea. Beth stared at its face. "The man-in-the-moon lies on his side in Brazil," she said. "In New Zealand he's upside down."

Leonardo, still holding her hands, looked up at the sky. "I never knew that."

Beth laughed. "Cool, eh?"

The season for burning

Simone had asked *seu* Pedro to bring Marcus this morning to help him lift the cover off the drain to find the source of the smell. But *seu* Pedro arrived for work alone and agitated. He filled the frame of the kitchen door, shaking his head from side to side like a wounded bull, and told us Marcus had fled to Rio. After five months in Brazil my Portuguese was just good enough to understand the gist of what he was saying.

"His case comes up next week, *dona* Simone. Everybody is after him, police, lawyers. Maria sold the fridge yesterday to give him the money for the bus. She was crying all night. I don't want to leave her alone today, so, if you don't mind, I'll just rake the leaves off the grass and go home." Still rolling his head he ambled off towards the shed, muttering, "*Meu Deus, meu Deus!*"

"Don't worry about the leaves, *seu* Pedro," Simone called after him. "Go home whenever you want. And please take the wedding present with you when you go. It's on the table in the kitchen." Turning to me she explained, "Last year Marcus shot someone."

"Shot?"

"Alcohol." She began peeling a papaya for her breakfast. "Well, tomorrow *seu* Pedro can find someone else to help him. We'll have to put up with the smell a little longer. When I designed this house I included a sewage treatment plant under the garden. My house is the only one in the area which does not have raw sewage running straight into the river." She ate a slice of papaya and looked out of the window. "Even though we've got politicians who get votes by promising to fill in rivers to make roads I believe that I, and others like me, can make a difference."

I asked her if leakage from the sewage could be causing the smell.

She pursed her lips. "I don't think so. Sometimes the girls from the *favelas* ..."

Isadora padded barefoot across the tiles towards us, unwinding a towel from her head. She shook out her long blonde hair with her hands. Shampoo and soap smells floated on the air. "What Simone is trying to say, Alexa, is that if they can't support another child, or if their father has made them pregnant or ..." Her sentence petered out as we heard the sound of hooves on the tarmac.

Through the window we saw the short, square figure of *dona* Antonia sliding off the back of her husband's horse. He watched her till she closed the gate behind her before he cantered off.

"What's happened to her bike?" I asked.

Simone rolled her eyes. "Her husband sold it to buy alcohol. She's very annoyed with him about that. But, as you see, Beth, even *dona* Antonia isn't prepared to walk alone in this neighbourhood. So you must not."

"But there's never anyone around," I protested.

"Well, of course they're not just waiting for someone to pass by, but if they see you with your camera taking pictures of this and that they will know you are a foreigner and they will assume you have money. Please at least wait until we can all go together."

This afternoon Isadora was busy overseeing the *pequena mostra de Rodin* in the *espaço cultural* in the new shopping mall. Rob and Beth had gone to help her. Isadora had talked of nothing else for weeks.

"In Uberlândia we don't have the facilities to show the originals. Only São Paulo and Rio got those. But even to obtain five replicas from the Rodin Boutique in Paris is good for our city. We're the first city in the interior to get them," she'd enthused.

Simone had gone with a team of environmentalists to the Miranda Valley, on the borders of Araguari, Uberlândia and Indianapolis. At the end of the year the valley would be flooded on the completion of the hydro-electric dam, so she was in the process of making a video and writing a book to record the flora and fauna before they disappeared.

I put *Caetano Veloso* on the CD player and lay in the hammock on the verandah watching the hummingbirds in the wild orchids Simone had brought back from her field trips. In Portuguese the word for hummingbird was *beija-*

flor – kiss flower. Beth loved the name so much she had given it to the foal we'd bought her for her seventeenth birthday. Beija Flor and his mum, Cristiane, lived on a farm owned by an American Agronomy professor called Bill. The deal I'd struck with Beth was that as soon as she'd finished her New Zealand Correspondence School work for the day she could spend the rest of the time on the farm with the horses. Bill was in the process of establishing a riding school for the disabled and Beth was helping him pick and train the horses.

At a barbecue the university had organised to welcome Rob into the engineering department, someone asked me if I'd give a talk about New Zealand to a group at the *Casa da Cultura*. She'd arrange a translator for me, she said. The translator was a woman called Rosalvina, from Panama, who'd completed her PhD in Linguistics in the USA, and was married to Bill, from the Agronomy department. Rosy invited us to her farm to meet Bill and their daughter Sally, who was Beth's age. Bill showed Beth his horses and pointed out a mare and foal that he was having trouble selling.

"Their owner was a kid of fifteen," he said. "Got knocked down and killed by a bus. Problem is no one can get near enough to that mare to catch her."

Beth took a rope off the barn door and strolled towards the horse. Bill's agronomy students followed, nudging each other. Every one of them had tried and failed to catch the horse. When Beth returned with the mare and foal they stared at her open-mouthed.

Rob whispered, "Her seventeenth birthday present?"

On another visit to the farm we met Simone, a colleague of Bill's from the Geography department. She inquired about our accommodation and when I told her how much we hated living in a sixteenth-floor apartment in the middle of the city, she said, as if it were the most natural thing in the world, "Then come and live with me! I have plenty of room in my house and my present tenant is moving out next week. My son is studying in Sao Paulo and I have only my friend Isadora living there with me, but she is often away in Sao Paulo too."

Isadora picked us up from the apartment that evening so we could look at the house. "You will love it there," she said. "It's outside the city and it's very peaceful."

She was right. In the month we'd been living here I loved waking up each morning to the sound of birds. In the evenings we often sat on the verandah in the gathering dusk, sometimes talking, sometimes listening to Simone and Isadora singing. One evening Simone sang *London London,* a song written by Caetano Veloso during his years of exile in England in the 1970s for singing protest songs about the military government.

"One day I will tell you about that terrible time in our history," she promised. "And about our own exile, my ex-husband's and mine."

Listening now to the melted-honey tones of Caetano I watched a flock of green and red parrots land screeching in the mango tree, dislodging a large green lizard. Yesterday, I'd seen a toucan there. But despite the music, the birds and the sun, the smell from the drain was too pervasive to ignore. I decided to go out and take some more photographs of the *cerrado*. Before leaving the house, I started writing a note for Rob and Beth in case they got back before I did, and noticed the quilt still on the table. It was a present from all of us for *seu* Pedro's youngest son who was getting married at the weekend. *Seu* Pedro had been too upset about Marcus that morning to remember to take it home. As I'd be going in the direction of his house I could drop it off.

Mindful of Simone's warning, I put my camera in a bag, jammed my sunhat on my head and drank two glasses of water before setting off, holding my breath as I closed the gate and stepped over the drain. A dozen scrawny white cows grazing on the scrub opposite the house stared at me. The little boy who looked after them each day was playing in a pile of sand by the big German-style house that was being built next door. His legs were deformed, so he was brought here each day on the back of a horse and cart by his older brother. *Seu* Pedro had told me that it was the child's job to stay with the cattle all day until it was dark, in return for food and shelter from his brother. At the same time Marcus had burst out with, "The way he treats Monstrinho he deserves to be strung up!"

"Monstrinho?" I said. "Why do you call him that?"

Marcus shrugged, "That's what everybody calls him."

Simone nodded. "The first time I heard them call him that I was shocked too, but this is how it is. The people in the *favelas* are protective of him, but he is so deformed they see him as a little monster." She went on to explain that the man also kept his young sister at home all day to clean and cook for him. "According to *seu* Pedro the last time he saw her she had a swollen belly. Who the father might be is anyone's guess."

I asked Simone if there was an agency in the city that could take the children out of that situation.

"Of course," she said. "I could ring up the social workers and report it. That man would go to prison for a long time, but these cases take so long to get to court that he could be on the loose for months. He'd have plenty of time to come here and kill me."

When she saw my expression, she sighed. "No, I'm not heartless, Alexa. But I can't take responsibility for all our social problems. The scale is too big. You haven't lived in Brazil long enough to understand."

Yesterday I had given the child a red T-shirt of Beth's. He'd put it on and smiled so widely that I could see the gaps in his back teeth. Simone said, "I doubt he'll be allowed to keep it." Today he was wearing his usual dirty, torn T-shirt over shorts that were three sizes too big and that he never seemed to change.

Now he was half-lying in the sand making roads in it with a stone. He must have been deeply engrossed in his game as he didn't look up when I came out the gate. His proximity to the drain made me wonder if he had something wrong with his nose as well as his legs.

"*Bom dia!*" I called out.

"*Bom dia,*" he replied without looking up.

I crossed over the road to climb the hill. The developers' plan for the old farmland on which Simone's house stood had been to establish a green belt outside the city, keeping the original trees in big gardens that could be seen from the road. The more environmentally sympathetic members of the City Council had pushed for by-laws to prevent property owners erecting high walls and cutting down trees. However, the lots had sold slowly. Despite the din and confusion of four hundred thousand people trying to live in a city that could barely accommodate half that number, buyers preferred the security of living downtown in tightly packed apartment buildings. The first few houses that had gone up began with low garden walls, but a couple of robberies had been enough to convince the owners that this concept couldn't work in Brazil and soon the by-laws were ignored and the walls became higher than the houses. The lots that had been bought since were mostly on land free of trees or with just a few that could be cut down easily. Simone's land had so many trees that nobody had been interested in it, so she had been able to buy it cheaply.

The garden provided a cool, shady refuge, but outside, in the scrub where cicadas fizzed like frantic telegraph wires, the heat was oppressive. Sweat began to pour down my back. There had been no rain for five months. The earth was like cracked terracotta.

Finally, I reached the top of the hill, which was the best vantage point to see the *cerrado*. But what I saw, lying by the side of the dusty road, were five dead horses. There were by-laws against dumping dead animals, but they were ignored. We never saw who dumped any of the rubbish that daily spread over the landscape, though Simone suspected the council rubbish trucks.

To the east the road led into dense scrubland. Twisted black *sucipira* trees and *buriti* palms stood against the glassy blue sky. To the west lay the city, the shining new high-rises obscured by billowing smoke. This was the season for burning. The green spaces that were not already covered with rubbish were rapidly being consumed by smouldering black. I never saw who lit the fires, though Simone said it was the small boys who tended the skinny cattle in the scrub. "They believe the grass will not come back in the spring if they don't burn it now. When I first came here I used to go out every day to put out the fires, but it was a waste of time. They just came back and lit them again."

To the north stood half a dozen big houses. The only garden visible from up here, apart from Simone's, belonged to her neighbour who owned a snake farm a few kilometres from the city.

"It's big business," Simone had explained, "extracting the poisons to make antidotes. She exports it to Switzerland. The house is stunning, and it was built entirely with snake poison."

Behind the house there was an even bigger one that looked like a fortress. Shards of broken glass glinted along the tops of the walls. The only way in was through remote-controlled iron gates. The wealth of this family came from farming emus to provide feathers for the Rio

Carnival. Simone had told me that six months ago robbers had hidden in the bushes till the gates opened to let the car out and held up the driver with guns. They'd stripped the entire house and the family was left tied up for two days until the driver managed to break free and call the police.

"They were lucky not to have been shot," said Simone. "Nobody knew what was happening because of those high walls. That's why I refuse to listen to my friends who tell me I am crazy for letting my house remain visible from the road."

The river, the *Lagoinha*, was the colour and smell of diarrhoea. According to the local newspaper at least one corpse per week was fished out of that river.

"The statistics show that we have more murders per week in this city than you have in New Zealand in one year," Simone told me. "Most of my colleagues live in the city and they would never go near the *favelas,* but actually most of those murders are the results of fights between the families who live there."

I held my hand over my nose and mouth as I crossed the bridge and headed south, where, behind the ragged banana trees the *favelas* huddled. The better houses were made of concrete and brick; others were sheets of tin and plastic over sticks. And there, incongruously juxtaposed in the middle of the dusty crossroads, like an arty advertisement in a glossy magazine, lay a bottle of white wine, a bunch of red roses and a large black chicken, its legs splayed out through the bow of red ribbon tied around the lacy wrapping paper.

Occasionally I saw rings of burning candles on crossroads at night or woke to the sound of drums, but this was the first sign of *macumba* I'd seen up close. The city newspaper was presently full of reports of negotiations between the Council and the leaders of Afro-Brazilian cults. The Council wanted to develop the scenic potential of the local rivers and waterfalls and was afraid that *macumba* offerings would frighten away the tourists. I checked to see that I wasn't being observed then knelt down to take a photograph. Simone would have been horrified if she'd seen me.

The morning after we'd moved into her house I opened the shutters and saw, on the branch of the mango tree over my bedroom window, the shape of a supine woman with a stake through her heart. Her face was contorted. When I told Simone this she asked me to show her. We stood looking at the branch.

Twisting her hands together she said, "I don't know Alexa. It's not that I'm superstitious, but I believe it's better not to focus on these things." And she led me away to the main trunk of the tree and asked if I could see the old owl that lived there. I wouldn't have seen him if he hadn't turned his head at that moment. Simone said, "Many people here believe owls are like guardian spirits. I prefer to focus on those things."

The quilt I carried to *seu* Pedro's house wasn't heavy, but it was awkward to carry up the pot-holed track to his house. A horse-drawn cart piled high with old newspapers lurched past, sending up a screen of red dust and scattering half a dozen chickens. I stumbled into a hole in the road and a group of barefooted children playing in the earth ran over to help me. Two of them carried the quilt and three others dashed off to alert *seu* Pedro. The sixth child walked beside me, pointing out the holes so I could avoid them.

Within minutes *seu* Pedro appeared at his door. When he saw me he gave a yelp of surprise and ran forward to shake my hand and direct the children to take the quilt into the house. He led me along a narrow alley to the back of the house. His was the best house in the street and, until yesterday, the only one that contained a fridge. A sheet of iron extending from the kitchen to an outhouse formed a roof over the small concrete yard which served as a dining room with a wooden table and four chairs. Two young girls were cooking rice on a woodstove while another sat at a table breast-feeding a baby. She looked up shyly as *seu* Pedro introduced her as his niece. I noticed a large purple bruise over her left eye.

"She was going out with a forty-year-old man," said *seu* Pedro in explanation. "When her mother found out they were having sex she said they had to get married. The judge wouldn't do it because she wasn't yet fourteen. So the man made her pregnant and then the judge agreed to marry them. But now ..." He spread his palms outward "... she has come here to live with us."

Dona Maria scuttled out of the kitchen wiping her hands on her apron. I already knew from Simone that *seu* Pedro had just finished building his wife a kitchen and had installed a new gas cooker, but to his intense frustration she didn't want to mess it up by cooking on it, so she continued to cook on the old wood stove in the outhouse. He repeated this story to me now, and added, as if to explain his wife's attitude, "She is one of twenty-two children."

Dona Maria glared at him. "Don't exaggerate! There were only twenty of us!"

I asked her how many had survived.

"Half," she said. "Only the girls, but thanks be to God they all have husbands."

I told her I was sorry about Marcus and asked what he would do in Rio.

"We have relatives there," said *seu* Pedro, glancing at his wife.

I watched *dona* Maria's hands smoothing a pink crocheted cover over the new gas cylinder on the bench. It perched there like a snugly fitting hat.

When I got back to Simone's house, the smell was even worse than when I'd left. The searing heat of the afternoon had hastened the decomposition of whatever was in the drain and the stench coated my throat with a thick, sickly layer that made me gag. Through a gap in the hedge I could see Rob, Beth, Isadora and Simone sitting on the verandah with a bottle of wine. Couldn't they smell it from there? Lamplight softly lit the interior of the house. A small, dry cough close by made me jump. Crouched in the shadows, the boy was still waiting for his brother to take him home. He looked up as I approached.

"*Boa noite,*" I said.

"*Boa noite,*" he replied, smiling this time.

Encouraged, I asked him his real name.

"*Monstrinho,*" he answered.

"I mean your *real* name?"

Silence.

I asked, "Where's your red T-shirt?"

Still no response, so I said, "See you tomorrow then," and opened the gate. As I locked it behind me I heard a horse and cart. The child's brother, wearing the red T-shirt, jumped down and lifted him onto the cart. He muttered something and gestured towards the drain. The boy looked round and nodded. Hidden behind the trees I watched them until they disappeared into the dusk.

I looked across the garden at Beth and stood quietly, observing her beautiful young face. She was listening intently to Simone.

"When my ex-husband was a student he was arrested three times for protesting against the military government. The Presbyterian Church arranged for us to escape to the USA to work on a political magazine informing people what was going on in South America. We were full of love and idealism. Our first child was born there. When our visa expired, we went to Chile, the only country in South America not under military government. A year later there was a coup. So, once more, we escaped, this time back to

Brazil. I was pregnant again. My husband had to hide until there was an amnesty."

A firefly darted across the garden flashing its light like a bright eye winking in the darkness. After a long silence Simone spoke again. "When we designed this house we wanted it to have the best features of the most beautiful places we'd ever lived in. It was the realisation of a dream. Our sons were almost through high school; my husband had the job he wanted; I began my PhD and started campaigning in local politics and formed a Green party. Everything was perfect."

"And then?" prompted Rob.

"And then my husband fell in love with a girl half his age."

Isadora shrugged. "This is why I don't want to marry."

"I don't regret my marriage," continued Simone. "I have my two boys. Roberto went to live in the USA because he couldn't endure the shame of the divorce. Frederiko would have gone too, but he wasn't fortunate enough to have an American passport."

"And what about you?" asked Beth.

"Me?" Simone's voice lifted again. "I committed myself to saving the *cerrado*. When it is withered and scorched, as you see it now, it seems inconceivable that anything could ever grow again. But the rains will come, the grass will grow and the flowers will bloom. There is always the *cerrado*."

The colour of sunshine

I called in to see *dona* Antonia yesterday in response to her invitation to drop by any time to take photographs of the house. I found her in the kitchen making soap.

"*Meu Deus, dona Alexa!*" she'd protested, pointing to her stained T-shirt and torn cycling shorts. Reluctantly she'd let me watch her stirring the thick brown concoction of pork fat, corn and butter in a huge iron cauldron while ducklings and chicks scooted about the earth floor and kittens tore at a worn patch on the sofa in the living room, but nothing would induce her to let me take a photograph. She asked me to return the following day after she'd tidied the house and put on clean clothes.

This morning, as I picked my way down the pot-holed track, I saw Elane outside her front door, dancing to an American pop song on the radio. She waved at me and opened the door to let me in, then turned off the radio and dashed into the kitchen yelling for her mother.

While my eyes were adjusting to the darkness of the tiny room I almost stood on a duckling. It ran, squawking, under a sheet of torn, pink plastic nailed into the roughly plastered-over bricks above the entrance to *dona* Antonia's bedroom. On the bare wall a picture of Christ with long blonde hair and blue eyes gazed into the room. Today there were no chicken droppings on the floor and the worn patch on the sofa had been covered with a piece of pink sparkly material. The aroma of freshly brewing coffee filled the house.

Dona Antonia came to greet me wearing a pink sparkly top and white cycling shorts and carrying a toddler on her hip. She still looked dubiously at my camera but instructed Elane to pour two cups of thick sweet coffee and gestured to me to sit on the sofa. She explained the child was her grandson. "His mother has gone away, so now my son and grandson have come here to live with me. Davyson has to work. He doesn't know how to look after a child."

"This is Davyson's child?" I asked. "I thought he was only seventeen."

"He is," *dona* Antonia replied. "So is his wife. Well, now she's left him. She's gone to Rio to work as a prostitute." Seeing my expression she added, "She's a beautiful girl. She'll make a lot of money. Then she can give Lucio a better life. Who knows? One day she might even be able to buy a big house, like the one near *dona* Simone's. She's more beautiful than that woman was when she was Fabia's age."

"The emu farmer's wife?" I asked.

"Emus? Yes, now they farm emus, but that isn't why they have so much money. That woman was born in the *favelas* in Rio. She started off as a prostitute then married an old man who was head of a kidnapping ring. She used to kidnap the children of rich people."

I choked on my coffee.

She put the child on the floor and sat in a wooden chair opposite me, sipping her coffee.

"When I was younger I used to work in Rio as a maid. My employer was a very kind woman. She gave me her own clothes to wear and treated me like a friend. We were the same size and shape. People often commented how alike we were. Every month some parcels were delivered to her basement. It was part of my job to divide the parcel into smaller parcels. Then I had to take them to some addresses. She paid me three minimum wages to do this. Maids usually only got one."

"Drugs?"

She nodded. "I didn't know at first, but it made no difference when I found out. If I hadn't delivered them someone else would have and I had five children to support. Then she told me she was going away for a few weeks. Before she left she gave me some of her clothes and a bottle of hair dye and told me to dye my hair blonde, like hers."

The story was interrupted by a large, fat goat bursting through the door and charging across the room to Elane. She hugged it round the neck and planted a kiss on the end of its nose. Then she grabbed one of its teats and gave it a squeeze, asking me if we had goats in New Zealand. A white jet squirted across the room and landed on a kitten's face. Elane started pulling the goat outside, but it was reluctant to move. *Dona* Antonia stood up, scooped the child onto her hip again and pushed the goat from behind.

"Let's go out with her," she said, "or she'll just come back in again. She hates being alone."

I followed Elane, the goat and *dona* Antonia into the backyard which was almost completely occupied by a pen containing three enormous pigs. Seemingly oblivious to the smell, Elane stretched her arm into their enclosure and patted each one on the head. "This is Cintia, and Zulmira, and Helena."

I murmured appreciation of the pigs' size and condition and turned back to *dona* Antonia. "So then you wore her clothes and dyed your hair the same colour as hers?"

She nodded. "The resemblance was amazing. She told me I looked more like her than her own sister. I felt so proud. Before she went away she told me not to tell anyone she'd left Rio just to see how many people mistook me for her. When she came back she told me she'd kidnapped a seven-year-old boy and had taken him to a house in Uberlândia until his parents paid the ransom money. She showed me pictures of the house, the child, and told me everything that happened there, that's how much she trusted me. It was the house we were talking about, *dona* Alexa. The woman who owns the house was her friend."

"But, *dona* Antonia …"

She shrugged. "I prayed to God to forgive me if I had done something wrong. Then I didn't have a bad conscience about it no more. God understands how it is for poor people." She reached into a box and yanked a protesting duck out by the wing. Underneath it lay half a dozen eggs. She instructed Elane to take them into the house.

"My husband had gone to Brasilia to find work and he was supposed to send for me. When he didn't, I thought about staying in Rio, but it's not easy to live there without a husband. My employer offered me more money to stay with her, that's how much she liked me. I was so tempted because I could have had a nice life with her, but I had my children to consider and they needed their father. Finally, I saved up enough money to pay for two seats on a bus to Brasilia. I had all my children with me. My friend Maria came too, with her three children."

"Two adults and eight children all the way to Brasilia? What a nightmare!"

"It was terrible," she laughed. "The journey took three days. Some of the children were teething and we didn't get any sleep. But when we arrived it was even worse because we had no idea where to start looking for my husband. Some people from the Spiritist Church took us to a place for homeless people and there we found my brother, Pedro. I hadn't seen him for about four years and I didn't even know he was in Brasilia. I found a job as a maid and saved up some more money while my brother looked for my husband. Then he found him. And do you know, *dona* Alexa," her voice cracked with indignation, "he was living with another woman!"

I shook my head in sympathy. "So what did you do?"

She roared with laughter. "I'm not very tall, but you might have noticed I'm a lot fatter than him! I pushed him to the floor and sat on him and threatened to smother him until he promised to get rid of that woman and come home with me."

I couldn't help laughing. "But why did you want him, after that?"

"I had five children. Who else would want to marry me? And why should I let another woman have my husband?" she responded in astonishment. "So he came back to me. Then Maria married Pedro. Her first husband had been shot in a fight before her last child was born and she needed another husband. Pedro had leprosy and the Spiritist Church sent him to the hospital in Uberlândia to get cured. When I came to visit him I saw how beautiful it was here, so we all came to Uberlândia to live beside him. Now most of my family live in this street. I thank God every day for my life, *dona* Alexa. I have my home, my family, my job at *dona* Simone's. My life would be perfect if my husband didn't drink. He spends all my money on drink so I can't save. And if I don't give him money he says he'll hang himself."

"No, *dona* Antonia," I protested. "He only says that to frighten you."

"He's done it twice already! The last time he'd already turned blue by the time we cut him down. I thank God every day that I still have a husband."

★

Dona Antonia's neighbour, a gaunt-looking man that I couldn't help thinking I wouldn't like to meet in a dark alley, stood scratching his bristly black hair while I explained how to use the camera. A swarm of children appeared out of nowhere and stood watching us, grinning, while we arranged ourselves into a group for the photograph. I beckoned them over to join us and after waving everyone into position the neighbour took the picture. And disappeared into his house with my camera. I glanced anxiously at *dona* Antonia, but she appeared not to have noticed. A few seconds later the man re-appeared with the camera in a plastic bag. He handed it to me with a warning not to have it visible on my way back home and before I could thank him, he strode back into his house.

I turned to say goodbye to *dona* Antonia, but now she too had disappeared. She returned with a bar of her homemade soap. "When you saw me making this yesterday it looked so brown and ugly, didn't it? But now see how beautiful it is!" She held it up to the light.

"It looks like a piece of sunshine," I said.

She laughed, "Sunshine? No!" and dropping the soap into the plastic bag with the camera, told me where I would find an *ipê* tree in bloom on the way back home. "Those flowers are the colour of sunshine, *dona* Alexa, not my old soap, but they blossom only once a year and the flowers last only a week."

The route she described to me was the place that led to the dumping ground for dead horses. As I approached the area, I persuaded myself that the smell couldn't be much worse than the pigs. But I was wrong. The stench of putrid flesh whacked into my lungs as if I'd charged into an invisible brick wall. I lifted my t-shirt and covered my nose and mouth with it, retching. In the same moment I saw the *ipê*. Incredibly, the fires, which were still smouldering in the charred grass, had not destroyed the tree. Trying hard not to breathe, I knelt down in the dust to take photographs, the horses in the foreground, the tree behind, its huge yellow flowers glowing like miniature suns.

From the top of the hill, above the dead horses, I could see the house that belonged to the emu farmers. The gates were sliding open to let a silver Mercedes out and as they closed again a guard jumped out of the car, holding a gun. After a minute he spoke into a mobile phone. A smaller gate beside the main one opened and another guard appeared holding the hand of a small girl. Both guards got into the car with the child and it sped away. Simone had explained that this elaborate routine was a precaution against the child being kidnapped. "They are worried that something might happen to their daughter," she said. "Kidnapping rich children is very common in Brazil." I watched the car until it disappeared.

The red and gold of the sky was fading and clouds of mosquitoes were already gathering in the shadows. The light wouldn't last long and Simone would be worried if I wasn't home before dark. I slung the camera over my shoulder and began to hurry through the scrub, keeping my eyes on the ground in case I surprised a snake.

I didn't see the shack until I was almost on it. They were springing up everywhere. Three others had appeared near the river last week and one evening we had seen a family washing themselves under a waterfall. Within days the banks were littered with the ubiquitous plastic bags and beer cans. Simone had already called the city council three times but bureaucracy moved so slowly that action was unlikely to be taken until several families had become well established and by then it would be too late to move them. "We'll end up with just as many *favelas* as São Paulo and Belo Horizonte," Simone had complained. "Soon there will be nowhere in Brazil where it's safe to live."

In front of the shack a man was sitting cross-legged on the ground eating from a tin bowl with his hand. He looked up as I approached. I nodded and walked by quickly. He pointed to my camera and gave a shout. My mouth went dry. I'd read the murder statistics. Listened to Simone's warnings. Seen *dona* Antonia riding to work on a horse. Accepted her neighbour's gift of a plastic bag to hide my camera. I wanted to run, but my legs wouldn't work. Then I realised he was waving his hand in the direction I'd come from. "*Olha alí.*"

I followed his gaze to an enormous mango tree where two toucans were just landing.

"*São bonitos, ne?*" He pointed to my camera and the birds, his face split by a toothless grin.

My hands were still shaking so much I could hardly adjust the focus on my camera as I framed the toucans and shot several pictures. When I looked at the man again he was once more bent over his bowl.

"*Obrigada,*" I thanked him.

"*Não tem problema,*" he said, intent on his meal.

I had one shot left. I asked if I could take a picture of him. He looked up, glanced at his surroundings and shook his head, his expression like *dona* Antonia's the day I'd caught her making soap.

Pablo's hair

The war between me and Pablo started the day Dad took me to Bill's farm to look at a horse he wanted to buy me for my birthday. Bill told us the mare had belonged to a kid who'd been killed when the bus he was holding onto to pull him and his bike up a hill, rolled backwards.

"A lot of kids are wiped out that way," Bill said. "You'll find things are a bit different here, Beth."

I'd already figured that out. On our way to the farm we'd got flagged down by the Military Police. This real mean-looking guy with a gun in his belt and boots up to his armpits made Bill get out of the car and asked to see his documents. Bill stuck out his chin and growled, "I'm not a horse. I don't carry my pedigree around with me."

I'd only lived in Brazil a few months, but it was long enough to know that nobody messes with the Military Police. To my surprise, the guy just muttered something and waved us on.

"Wow, your dad's something!" I whispered to Bill's daughter, Sal.

She said it was only because they'd realised Bill was an American and they didn't want to make trouble for themselves. Bill added that the Military Police liked to stop people on the pretext of checking documents just to get bribes and you had to let them know who was boss. Fine. So why didn't he let Pablo know who was boss?

When we got to the farm Bill explained that the dead boy's parents had asked him to keep the pregnant mare and her two-year-old colt till they found a buyer, but none of the guys who came to look at her could even catch her.

"Don't worry, Beth," he reassured, "I've asked Pablo to do a bit of schooling so she'll be calm enough for you to ride."

We turned the corner into the barn and saw the colt tied to the fence. His mother, a beautiful bay, was tied to a pole while Pablo, sweat soaking into his red bandanna, laid into her with a whip. The mare was foaming at the mouth and you could see the whites of her eyes as she galloped round and round in terror.

I stopped dead in my tracks. "You call this schooling?"

Dad flashed me the look he reserves for when I open my mouth before I get my brain into gear.

Bill explained that he was starting a riding school, so it was important that the horses were quiet and well-trained.

"Yeah, right," I shot back, "like that's going to happen if you let Pablo loose on them. Tell him to untie her."

Dad told him it was okay, so Bill said something in Portuguese to Pablo. The minute Pablo untied the mare she tore out the barn like there was a lion on her back. I grabbed a lead rope and followed her with everybody running behind me. When the mare got to a safe distance she started grazing. I approached her real slow, talking to her all the time. After a few minutes she let me stroke her shoulder. After another minute I slipped the rope around her neck and walked her back to the barn. By now half a dozen of Bill's agronomy students had wandered over. They were all looking at me like, "What planet do you come from?"

Dad said if I wanted the mare she was mine. I asked Bill what her name was.

"Cristiane," he said. "Her colt doesn't have a name yet."

A thumb-sized hummingbird buzzed in front of my face before diving into a flower.

"What's the name for hummingbird in Portuguese?" I asked.

"*Beija-Flor*," Sal said. "It means kiss-flower."

I stroked the colt's mane. "Hi *Beija-Flor*," I whispered in his ear.

After we bought Cristiane and Beija-Flor I rode at the farm every weekend. When Bill saw the way I rode he asked me to go to a horse auction to help him pick out some decent horses for the riding school.

We chose three beauties, a grey, a chestnut and a roan. Bill said I could name them. The roan was very close to foaling and she reminded me of my first pony, Gloria, so that one was easy. Then I offered to come every day to train them all. Bill whistled between his teeth and said he had to be careful not to offend Pablo, who was still smarting over the Cristiane episode. For once I did get my brain into gear before voicing my opinion about Pablo.

I saved this for Sal, a few days later, after we'd watched Gloria's new foal stagger up off the straw on his matchstick legs and take his first drink.

"We'll leave them to get acquainted," said Bill, ushering us out of the paddock and closing the gate. "I'll have Pablo check them over this afternoon." Seeing my expression he grinned and said, "But you can choose his name."

"Glorious," I said. "Son of Gloria."

"Perfect," said Bill.

Sal and me headed over to the farmhouse to have a game of volleyball. "*Pablo* check them over?" I began, incredulously. "Personally, I wouldn't let that moron anyway near …"

My sentence was interrupted by an explosion of swearing from inside the farmhouse and Pablo's goat flew out the front door on the end of someone's foot. Pablo's head poked over the top of the pigsty. When he understood the reason for the racket he came lumbering out, scratching his neck. The goat saw him and bounded over as if it was about to fling itself on his chest in pure joy. Even at that distance the pong was enough to singe a layer or two off your tonsils. Pablo grabbed it by the horns and dragged it towards us.

Me and Sal started gagging. It did no good though. "What stink?" he always said when we whinged about the goat. He tied it to a tree.

"Why can't you take him into the pigsty with you?" Sal complained.

"Because I'm chopping up a stillborn calf for the pigs," he answered, sliding his eyes across at me.

When Sal translated this I gagged again, this time for real. His face split into a grin like a sliced melon and he went swaggering back to the pigsty, hoiking and spitting.

"He hates me," I snivelled.

"Nah. He's jealous of you," Sal said. "The other day he was trying to catch the new Appaloosa and it kept running away from him and one of the guys said, 'Let Beth do it'."

"Yeah?"

"But then Pablo said it wasn't a job for girls, especially skinny snooty up-themselves white girls from a country nobody's even heard of." She hooted with laughter at the expression on my face.

I watched the top of his bandanna bob up and down behind the wall in the sty. That bandanna was probably red because it was saturated with blood. Nobody'd ever seen Pablo without it. I bet he even slept in it.

Once, Sal dared me to ask him why he never took it off and he said it was because he had this real thick curly hair and it was difficult to keep it clean with his work on the farm, but Sal and me had our suspicions. Soon after that we saw him dive in the lake and swim underwater all the way to the other side. When he climbed out he was completely starkers, but his bandanna was still grafted in place. He stood still for a minute, just gazing over the water, looking like one of those huge termite mounds that were all over the farm.

The fumes from the goat made us abandon any idea of playing volleyball and in two minutes we were out of gassing range and heading back to the barn.

Beija-Flor came up to me and stuck his nose in my neck. I decided to ask Dad if we could ship him and Cristy back to New Zealand when Dad had finished his contract here. I sure didn't want them to end up as street horses pulling carts of rubbish and being flayed with sticks to run faster and faster when they were exhausted and thirsty and the sun was blazing down on their poor mangy coats. Cristy plodded over to me and breathed in my face. For the millionth time I made a wish that I could be with her when her foal was born. Then I blew my breath back into her nostrils.

She was bleeding from three new cuts and was covered with ticks again. "Gross, eh?" I said to Sally, picking one off and bursting it between my fingernails. Over the squawking of the guinea fowl that started fighting for the ticks we chucked at them, I heard Bill's voice and saw him and two of his students, João and Roberto, trudging across the paddock to the barn.

The guys said something to Sal and she translated, "João wants Roberto to race you. He says he's going to bet all his money on you."

Sal thought Roberto was cute, but I didn't like his voice. He sounded like Donald Duck.

He said, in pretty good English, "I've got some cream for you, Beth. You spread it on the cuts and when those vampire bats drink the blood it gets on their feet. Their friends lick it off and it poisons them all."

I made a face. "I hope it's a quick death."

Bill said, "The other horses are looking pretty good Beth, since Pablo's been treating them with that cream. It's only your two the bats are after now."

"Okay," I said, "but I don't want Pablo anywhere near my horses. I'll put the cream on myself. I'll get Dad to drop me off every day. I could break in the new Appaloosa for you at the same time," I added hopefully.

Bill sucked in air through his teeth, "Sure, if you can get Pablo to agree to making you an honorary guy."

Roberto and João cracked up.

I glanced at Sal, who rolled her eyeballs.

Bill took his glasses off and rubbed them on his shirt. "Honey, we've just been looking at that new foal. One of the other horses must've kicked him. His leg's broken."

"Glorious?" I said in disbelief.

He nodded.

My mouth went dry. "But he's just been born. Are you going to shoot him?"

"I don't have a gun, Beth. Pablo'll have to whack him on the head with an axe."

My face went as green as the tick I was holding.

Bill said, "It'll be quick. Pablo'll know what to do."

"Speaking of the devil," Sal muttered.

I looked up to see Pablo sauntering towards us with his parrot, Rosa, squawking in his ear.

Bill told him about the foal. Pablo listened, staring at the ground, scratching his head. If I walked out, he'd see my green face. No way would I give him that pleasure. Bill said he'd know the exact spot to hit the foal, but what if he missed? Beija-Flor stuck his nose in my ear. I was grateful for the excuse to bury my face in his mane.

There was a long silence. Then Pablo coughed and said, "We could donate him to the veterinary school. Give him a chance."

I lifted my head from Beija's neck and looked at Bill, biting my lip. Bill rubbed his chin.

"I'll ring them," he said at last, half-running in the direction of the house. Pablo lumbered after him with Rosa perched on his head like a tattered wedding hat.

Nobody uttered a word. Then Roberto cleared his throat and said, "He found Rosa when she'd just hatched. Her mother was dead near the nest. Dogs probably. Pablo took her home and raised her."

I watched Pablo disappear into his shack.

"So what about that race?" said Roberto.

He didn't really sound like Donald Duck.

"I'll let you ride Skewbald," I said. "I'll take Madonna."

"You nuts?" said Sal. "If she went any slower she'd be dead."

After the race we cantered back to the barn, laughing and yahooing. Bill looked up from the saddle he was cleaning. I waved at him. He'd know from my grin that I'd won again. But his face was the colour of putty. I vaulted off the horse in one movement. "The vet school said no, didn't they?"

"I'm sorry honey. So Pablo had to …"

Sal burst into tears. The guys got very busy unsaddling. I ran out the barn with my hand over my mouth and bent over in the long grass near the henhouse and puked.

I lay there for a minute, letting the sun warm my cold skin, trying not to think of Pablo feeding bits of the foal to his disgusting pigs. Oh, wouldn't he just love that! I squeezed my eyes tight and hit the earth with the side of my hand pretending it was Pablo I was chopping up into little pieces. Then I bawled my eyes out.

When I was all cried out I hauled myself up and wiped the snot off my face. My body smelt sour, like cheese left out in the sun. The air burned and stung and crackled. Two swallow-tails flew low over the baked red earth and skimmed the surface of the lake. Yeah, I'd go for a swim and try to feel clean again. As I trailed past the hen-house I heard a high-pitched wheezing coming from inside. I back-tracked and peered through a gap in the planks. Pablo was sitting on a box that was covered with chicken shit, wiping his nose with his bandanna and breathing like he was having an asthma attack. But it wasn't the sight of the tears glistening in the black leathery cracks of his cheeks that stopped my breath. It was his head. As bald and shiny as a light bulb.

The night of the goddess

Beth was taking notes under the shade of a banana tree while Marcia explained the process of making *pamonhas*. As I approached the cooking area the acrid smell of pigshit wafted up from the pigsty on a wave of hot air. Marcia shooed a squawking chicken away from her feet, shoved another log under the woodstove and flicked her hand at the thick, black clot of flies crawling over the dish of boiled corn and pork fat.

"If I get an A for this it'll be yours," said Beth, in not-too-bad Portuguese.

Marcia grinned, showing a gap where her front teeth were missing. "Why would anyone in your country want to know how I make *pamonhas*?"

"It's for Correspondence School," said Beth. "I have to write about a local product. I went to a few shops in town that sold *pamonhas*, but they wouldn't tell me how they made them."

"They were probably scared you would use their recipe and set up shop for yourself," laughed Marcia. "Now, if you want to write about something interesting I'll take you to the *Festa de Iemanja* tonight. We can easily walk to the lake from here."

"That'd be cool, wouldn't it Mum?" said Beth, still in Portuguese.

I nodded, turning my head to hide my pleasure that she found it natural to talk in this language that she'd been so resistant to learning.

Marcia scooped up a spoonful of the yellow mixture to pour inside an envelope of corn leaves which she fastened up with string and threw into a pot of boiling water. Plucking a corn leaf envelope from another pan she cut it open with a pair of scissors, put it on a plate, handed it to Beth with a fork then proceeded to prepare one for me. Beth paled slightly, but she ate it without comment. Marcia wiped her hands on her faded cotton dress. Three small girls, their bare feet stained red from the earth, ran in to the kitchen and clung to her legs laughing. She gave them a *pamonha* each then shooed them outside along with the piglet that was following them.

"Where's your father?" I asked Beth.

"Out with Antonio looking for snakes. They lost a calf yesterday from snake-bite," she said. "They even took Ricardo with them, so it can't be as lethal out there as you seem to think!"

"Ricardo is used to this terrain; you're not."

She rolled her eyes. "Oh Mum! You have to stand on a snake before it attacks you. That's why the calf got bitten. They don't just come charging after you for no reason. It'd be so cool to see a snake!" She turned to Marcia. "We don't have snakes in New Zealand."

Marcia looked incredulous and began to tell us snake stories of her childhood. "One day I'd been swimming naked and I ran to the toilet because I had diarrhoea. From the corner of my eye I saw lots of lines on the ground headed in the direction I was going, but I was so worried that I wasn't going to make it to the toilet in time that I took no notice. Then I got there and opened the door and ..." Her hands sprang open at the memory. "... the place was on the point of bursting with snakes. They were hanging down from the ceiling. They covered the floor. They were even coiled around the loose planks on the walls. I forgot the diarrhoea and ran all the way back to the house hollering my head off. I wanted my mother, but the house was full of people because my uncle had just died and everybody had come to pay their respects. They stood around his coffin, staring at me with their eyes on stalks, their mouths wide open as I ran naked and screaming through the house!"

As Marcia and Beth bent double, shrieking with laughter, I shuddered, unable to extract a shred of humour from the story. When Marcia's laughter subsided a little I asked her if they kept antidotes on the farm. Wiping tears from her eyes, she shook her head. "No, no, they're too expensive."

"But you let Ricardo go snake-hunting?"

She shrugged. "This is his life. He has to learn how to deal with it."

Beth gazed at the row of little T-shirts drying on the length of barbed wire that stretched from the kitchen to the pigsty. "Why do you stay here, Marcia?"

"Where else should I go?" she responded. "This is my home. There is even a bus that takes Ricardo to school. I had only one year of school and my husband has never been to school. All my children are healthy here, even though three out of the four are girls." She glanced at me. "And Antonio and me, we're trying to make another son. That will be my request to *Iemanja* tonight." She looked at Beth and back at me again. "It's good for a girl to have lots of brothers."

Before I could reply Beth jumped up from her seat and ran towards a cloud of red dust rising above the guava trees. Two vehicles appeared on the dirt road to the farmhouse. Neber, the owner of the farm, stepped out of the first car with his son Fabricio. His wife, Fernanda, stepped out of the second with four of her nephews. They lived in another city and only came here at weekends. Antonio managed the place the rest of the week. Fernanda said something to the boys and they all came over to shake our hands. They then stood in a line and kissed Beth on both cheeks.

Fernanda hugged me and said, "Can you believe that? I told them New Zealanders don't greet each other with a kiss and that Beth would be embarrassed, but look at them! They're exaggerating it!"

Beth's face was scarlet. The boys spoke to her in English and offered to drive her in the tractor to show her the waterfall and go for a swim.

"Maybe later," I intervened, "then we can all go together. The river down there is rough."

Beth rolled her eyes and Fabricio reassured, "Is no problem. I swim in the river all my life. Is safe."

He and Beth ran off towards the tractor shed.

Fernanda touched my arm. "Don't worry. They'll look after her. They'll be like her brothers."

Fabricio reappeared at the wheel of an ancient tractor to which the boys attached a rickety wooden cart. They jumped in, pulling Beth with them.

"You want to drive, Beth?" yelled Fabricio above the noise of the engine. "I show you."

"She can't …" I began as Beth clambered into the driver's seat. The tractor zig-zagged across the track, belching smoke and dust. Fernanda and Marcia nodded their approval.

"She doesn't have a licence," I said. But no one was listening.

We climbed out of Fernanda's car and stood on the hill looking at the waterfall boiling over the rocks. Two of the boys were already under it and two others were splashing in the pool further below. Beth was watching Fabricio swinging across the river on the end of a rope. When he landed he hurled the rope back to her. She grabbed it and launched herself across the churning white water. Fabricio caught her on the opposite bank. Their laughter bounced off the rocks. The sun slid through the thick canopy of leaves and fell in slices of green light onto the river. The empty rope dangled from its branch. I crossed my arms over my shoulders, hugging myself, shivering.

A large blue butterfly fluttered around Fernanda's head. She smiled at me. "There, now you can see they are safe. They're having fun. Let's leave them alone. They'll be back when they're hungry."

"The butterflies here are so beautiful," I murmured, to divert her scrutiny of my face. "In New Zealand we have only thirteen species, although there used to be forty."

She nodded. "Every time I come here, or go to some special natural place, I feel that I am an intruder, so I ask the spirits who guard the place for their permission to be present. When a blue butterfly appears and flies around me I know permission has been given."

I asked if she was going to the *festa*.

"No," she said, "I don't like *Umbanda*. I'm a Catholic."

"But you talk about nature spirits."

She laughed. "You would have to be Brazilian to understand."

A full moon hung over the lake. Hundreds of chanting women in hooped white lacy dresses and men in white tunics stood their lit candles in the sand at the water's edge.

Two men lifted the statue of the black Goddess from her litter and placed her in a small boat filled with flowers and burning candles. The image was clothed in blue and white robes like the Virgin Mary, but with voluptuous breasts and opulent hair. As she was towed around the lake groups of women and girls launched little paper boats filled with flowers and cosmetics.

"If the boats sink," explained Marcia, "it means *Iemanja* has accepted their gifts and will grant their requests."

The night filled with the sound of drumming; low, throbbing, hypnotic. People began dancing to the rhythm. I looked around anxiously for Beth. Two people near me began jerking their limbs. A group of elderly women gathered around them and hung beads and flowers around their necks and guided their steps. From time to time they fell to the ground, but were helped up to continue their dance. When the music stopped they stood still, swaying from side to side. Their faces were vacant, like the faces of the dead.

I shivered and Marcia put her arm around me. "It means the saint has descended," she explained. "That's good. They will be filled with the energy of their saint." She took my hand and guided me through the mass of dancers to the edge of the lake.

"Now I will make my request to *Iemanja*." She bent down and sent her boat of flowers out onto the water. It bobbed on the surface for a moment until the paper became saturated, then keeled over on its side and slipped beneath the surface. Marcia clapped her hands together and laughed aloud. "That means she has agreed to send me a son to replace Lucio."

"Lucio?"

"My firstborn. He died a year ago."

I drew in a sharp breath. "I had no idea."

She touched my arm. "Beth asked me not to tell you. He was bitten by a snake."

"Couldn't you get him to a hospital in time?"

She shook her head. "When we found him he was already dead, bleeding from his eyes."

We stood in silence on the sand, watching garlands of flowers floating on the lake. The cool water slapped over my bare feet. My nostrils filled with the smell of cooking fish, my ears with drumming and singing and laughter. I searched for words, but could find none.

A group of young girls approached us, so intent on their dancing they didn't see us and one of them fell against me, knocking me off balance and pitching me forward onto the sharp pebbles at the water's edge. A jagged pain stung my knees and the palms of my hands. The girls helped me up, the one who pushed me apologising profusely, her face stricken. She took her garland of white orchids from around her neck and thrust it into my hands. I called after her to tell her it was okay, she needn't part with her flowers, but she was already gone. A gap appeared where she had melted into the crowd and I thought I saw Beth dancing with Fabricio. The gap closed again so quickly I wondered if I'd imagined it. I looked at the flowers I was holding and saw they were smeared with blood from my torn hands.

Marcia tut-tutted. "Those clumsy girls! Look what they've done!" With her hand under my elbow she led me into the lake until we were wading knee-deep. "Put your hands in the water."

"Marcia, it doesn't matter …" I began, looking around for Beth in the mass of dancers.

She took my hands. "This is her life. Let her live it."

Then she bent down and cupped her own hands in the lake, letting the water trickle from them over my bleeding palms. She did this until all the blood was washed away. The garland of flowers slipped from my fingers. It drifted on the water until the flowers separated and floated out of sight.

New Zealand

2002 – 2003

The bough breaks

A blackbird's wing on the steps of Riccarton House is all it takes to stop me in my tracks. Through the window I can see a slight, grey-haired woman addressing a roomful of people. I can't believe I let Marianne talk me into this. But before I have a chance to bolt Marianne materialises in the doorway.

Her warm hands on my cold skin.

"Okay, just for today," I say. "Not tomorrow though."

She pats my shoulder and leads me into the house, through the oak-panelled hall lined with animal heads, to a seat at the back of the crowded drawing-room where the woman I'd seen through the window is talking to the audience about the stages of grief.

"Dr Claudia Drashe," Marianne whispers. "Trained under Elizabeth Kubler-Ross who pioneered the study of dying. The short man sitting on the left is Simon, the channel for Shulgi."

I look at Marianne and raise one eyebrow.

"Just keep an open mind."

Once, as a teenager, I'd persuaded my aunt to let me come to one of her Spiritualist circles. She only agreed when I promised not to breathe a word to my mother, who, my aunt said, would never speak to her again if she found out. I don't know what my imagination had conjured up about how a medium should look, but the woman in my aunt's darkened living room was definitely not it. This Dame Edna Everage clone peered over her purple-framed glasses at the old man beside me and boomed, "I see a woman behind you, Sir. G ... I think her name has a G in it. Does that mean anything to you?"

"G? Oh! That must be Gladys! My wife had a sister called Gladys!"

"Well, Gladys wants to tell you she's worried about your blood pressure."

The old man sat up straight. "Me blood pressure? Pity she didn't worry about me soddin' blood pressure when she was alive, the spiteful old cow ..."

"Yes yes, she says she's sorry about that. She wants you to know she didn't know then what she knows now. She wants you to forgive her. She knows about your bad heart and wants you to watch your health."

"Me 'eart?"

"Yes, you see they watch over us from the world of Spirit, you see. She's saying 'God Bless' and giving you a kiss now before she leaves."

"A kiss? She bloody well ..."

"Bert? Bert? I have a Bert now – does anyone know a Bert ...?"

It was only my aunt's warning glare that kept me from bursting.

The audience claps and Claudia Drashe sits down. I realise that I haven't heard a word she has said. Simon stands now and moves to the front of the podium. Mid-thirties, tanned, T-shirt and jeans. He doesn't look like a medium either. He explains that Shulgi lived in Sumaria three thousand years ago and has a great sense of humour. We shouldn't be surprised, he says, when Shulgi starts telling jokes as that is one of his teaching tools. Several people in the audience nod. I stifle a sigh and focus on the wallpaper, curtains and carpet. They are, according to the guidebook, faithful reproductions of the originals.

Five years ago we took some visitors to dinner in the restaurant of the newly-refurbished Riccarton House, with a ghost tour by candlelight thrown in.

"I always ask Jane Deans' permission to enter these rooms," whispered the guide. "She put her heart and soul into this house."

A German tourist asked if the house was *really* haunted. In reply, the guide told a story about the birth of the last Deans in the house.

"When the infant's sister was taken to see him she inquired who the old lady was."

"What old lady?" asked the child's mother.

"The old lady in the long black dress and white cap, bending over the cradle," replied the child.

The tourists gasped. The guide smiled. Then slowly raised her candle to illuminate Jane Deans' photograph on the wall, in her black dress and lace cap.

After that tour I was so impressed with the renovations that I wanted to book the house for Olivia's wedding reception. Beth and Sam came with us to inspect it. As soon as Beth saw the stuffed bison and deer heads on the walls of the restored oak-panelled hall she said she would not be bridesmaid if the reception was held there. No amount of persuasion about the heads being part of the history of the house, the cultural climate of the past, would move her. Olivia said it wasn't worth the fight and we might as well go and book Mona Vale instead. That was just as romantic and the Avon River was right in front of the house so the bridal party could be carried by punt.

Beth hugged her.

"You owe me big time, little sister!" Olivia said. "Just wait till it's your turn."

"Who would have her?" muttered Sam.

"No way am I getting married!" Beth shot back. "Guys just slow you down."

"You say that now," said Olivia, "but you don't know what the future holds."

"I know that much."

It's coffee time and the seminar participants take their cups out onto the verandah and find a spot in the thin autumn sunshine. Others wander down to the river where the

Deans men had soaked the oak trees they'd grown from acorns brought from England, before cutting them into panels for the hall. Marianne is talking to Dr Drashe and I want to wait until she finishes so I can explain it was a mistake for me to come. This is the first time I've left home in a month so even the watery sunshine is too bright for my eyes. I put on my sunglasses and wander over to the little shack John Deans built for his bride, more than a hundred and fifty years ago.

I look through the windows at the tiny dark rooms, the old wooden cradle in the bedroom. What did Jane think the first time she saw her new home? The remnants of bush preserved in the garden covered much of the swamp in the Canterbury Plains when she first came here. Did she think it was worth her journey? In her letters home to Scotland she wrote only that the cottage was dark. Just before her husband died of tuberculosis a year later, she promised him she'd run the estate till their baby son was old enough to inherit it, and that she'd make sure the bush was preserved forever. Then she built the big house where her son raised his own children. Eleven children from her one child. Not all survived. There were many ways for children to die back then.

Twenty-five years ago I wrote to my mother describing Riccarton House and Jane Deans' cottage and the way a fantail had followed Olivia and Sam as they scrambled over fallen kahikatea in the bush and how the movements of my new baby felt like moths' wings inside my belly and how the guidebook said, 'Far away from home and pregnant. Those pioneer women were a breed apart.'

"Hello, I'm Anna."

The voice makes me jump. I turn to see a woman about my own age who'd been sitting in front of me at the seminar.

"Those early settlers, eh?" She points to the cradle in the tiny room.

I nod and she asks what brought me to the seminar.

But I still can't say my daughter's name and the word 'died' in the same breath. So I tell her, "I don't believe in channels or whatever they call themselves, so I won't be back tomorrow."

"That's a pity," she says. "I haven't seen Shulgi before, because Simon usually works in the North Island, but there's a woman here in Christchurch who channels a being called Kasra. Until I met Kasra I didn't believe in channels either."

I don't want to discuss beings called Shulgi or Kasra and as people are starting to drift back into the house I turn in that direction. There's no sign of Marianne. Maybe I'll leave now and ring her later to apologise. A sycamore leaf spirals down in front of us. Anna reaches out and catches it.

"The Deans planted wonderful trees," she says. "I love coming here in autumn."

I glance briefly at the deep red of a pin oak.

"You're English, aren't you?" she says.

"Yes."

"Me too. I found it hard enough only three decades ago to leave my mother and sisters on the other side of the world, so I don't know how Jane Deans did it."

"At least we have the internet now," I say, managing a smile.

"Oh, e-mails!" Anna laughs. "I couldn't have endured my daughter living overseas without them. An only child, you see."

I look at the ground.

"She had a flat in London, close to Regent's Park," Anna says, bending down to pick up an acorn. "When I went over there to bring her home, we went for a walk in the park and collected the brightest autumn leaves we could find. She gave me a book to press them in, a volume of poems by Ursula Bethell that she'd found in a second-hand bookshop in London. When I opened the book the first line I read was *Such and such an autumn was very golden, and everything is for a very short time.*"

"You brought her home?" I ask, curious now.

"Five years ago. Stomach cancer."

Absorbed with the acorn Anna doesn't see my expression as she describes the weeks of chemotherapy, the blonde wig that covered her daughter's bald head, the nausea and vomiting, the weight loss, the pain.

"Then one morning I woke up for no reason. I looked at the clock. It was 2am. I knew something was wrong." She pauses. "I looked for her in her room, but she wasn't there. I went out into the garden and found her. Hanging from a tree."

I stop, my breath ripped from my chest.

"When Riccarton House was restored, I thought it would be the perfect place to celebrate my daughter's 21st," she says. "Instead, we held her funeral here."

She studies the acorn and the sycamore leaf. "Before we closed her coffin I took the leaves we'd gathered in England and put them in her hands. A fantail flew into the room, circled around my head then flew back into the bush. The first time I went to see Kasra he told me about those leaves, and the bird. He couldn't have known. He couldn't possibly have known. But he did."

Simon – or Shulgi – is walking towards us. Towards me.

"I have to give you a hug," he says.

I take a step back. I don't want hugs from strangers. Or stories about poems and fantails and autumn leaves and girls hanging from trees. It hurts to breathe. But he's holding me. And he's saying, "You didn't need to pack away her music. Play her music again."

When I return next morning the sky looks bruised. The rain is turning to sleet. As I lock my car I see Anna struggling with a bright red umbrella. She sees me and hurries across the car park.

"You came back!" she says, holding the umbrella over us both. "If you hadn't, I'd've blamed myself."

"Why?"

She bites her lip. "It was that cradle in the dark little room, and the red and gold in the leaves. It all just spilled out … how could I have been so thoughtless? When I heard what Shulgi said … about her music … I couldn't sleep last night."

"It's all right," I soothe.

Her breath escapes.

I ask what her daughter's name was.

"Tamsin," she says. "And *your* daughter?"

I take a deep breath.

"Beth."

"Will you tell me about her?"

"I'll try," I say.

And we walk up the steps into Riccarton House.

Grit

Beth's twenty-fourth birthday. The sky is that dazzling blue of a Canterbury autumn day. Sunlight shimmers on the leaves of the pin oak, turning them into little crimson flames. Rob puts the green box on the earth next to the rowan tree. *"Rowan – Protector of Young Women,"* Beth had said a year ago, filing sketches for her Celtic Goddess project. The rowan tree is just a few centimetres high, but when it grows it will have a fine view of the mountains. We reach into the box and gather a handful of ashes. A truck hurtles down the gravel road, shattering the stillness, sending up clouds of dust. There's no wind yet, but later there'll be gusts, scattering red and gold leaves. We need to say her name, but we have no breath. I form its shape in silence. Let her name float on the wind. Let it drift like mist around the verandah posts, under the eaves of the house, in and out of the trees and bushes, over the paddocks where the sheep graze, down the road to the river, where the Alps shine against a brilliant blue, where the tracks are covered in orange poppies and wild purple lupins, where the air is filled with the humming of bees and the songs of larks, and the striking of hooves on stone.

And the girl on the horse turns. And looks at you with eyes as blue as the sky.

The ashes slip through our fingers under the rowan tree. I wonder why they're called ashes. They're not. They're grit. Pure grit.

Time to leave

Rob wanted to return to Brazil for his long-deferred sabbatical. His eyebrows shot up when I suggested the Middle East.

"Oman? It's on the border of Saudi Arabia! On the spectrum of societies, it's about as far away from Brazil as you could get."

Which was why I wanted to go. What was the point in chasing shadows?

Justin, a work colleague, had lived in the Gulf for five years and he said that although the money wasn't as good in Oman the lifestyle was better than in the UAE. The people weren't so arrogant, he said, because they didn't have as much oil and weren't so rich, and the country was politically stable. The present sultan had taken over from his father in 1970. In just thirty years under Sultan Qaboos, the capital, Muscat, had bloomed like a flower in the desert, and there was an ever-expanding modern infra-structure that linked the coastal and mountain villages. The government, well aware that the oil would run out in about forty years, was keen on educating the young, sending them to Australian and British universities and training them to take over the jobs from the ex-pats who'd been running the country for the past few decades. English Language teachers were in great demand.

"I'd give it a go if I were you," Justin had urged, scribbling the e-mail address of a friend of his. "Philippe Jouvellier. Nice guy. Canadian. We worked together for three years in Egypt. He went to Muscat last year to be the Director of Studies of a new private language school there."

"Thanks, I'll e-mail him," I said.

The offer of a job at *English for Life* came back by return e-mail. It sounded tempting. Airfares paid there and back, furnished accommodation, tax-free salary, allowance for petrol, and electricity, a fortnight's gratuity at the end of the twelve-month contract. New surroundings. New people. New energy. Rob reluctantly agreed it sounded okay. He had papers to write and his book to finish and a whole year doing just that might be a godsend. "No harm in contacting Sultan Qaboos University to see if they can offer me something," he said. "Though I've heard that when the American and European lecturers made a hasty exit after September 11, the university started replacing them with Arabs from Egypt and Jordan."

I accepted the job offer: twenty-five contact hours per week and only three weeks annual leave, but working long hours was what I wanted right now. I wrote to ask if there would be a problem in paying the gratuity if I took all my leave at the end of my contract which would mean, in effect, I'd leave after eleven months. No problem, Philippe assured. He'd checked with Hussein, the CEO. I asked if, instead of the school sending me a return air ticket, I could pay my own fare and be refunded when I got to Muscat as we wanted to go to the UK en route. No problem, though I should realise, Philippe warned, that it was the company's policy to give single tickets, not returns, but Hussein had told him I would be reimbursed for the cost of a single ticket from Christchurch to Muscat when I arrived in Oman, and at the end of my contract, the cost of a single ticket from Muscat to Christchurch.

Rob suggested we include a short trip to Brazil at the end of the contract, before returning to New Zealand. By then, he ventured, it might be okay to go back?

Colleagues were doubtful when I told them our plans.

"Oman?"

"Do they have public beheadings there?"

"What about stoning?"

"Will you have to wear a veil?"

"You won't be able to drink alcohol. Or eat pork."

"Stick a New Zealand flag on your car or they'll think you're Americans. They don't like Americans."

"Go through your contract with a fine-tooth comb."

"My brother's friend taught in Saudi and he couldn't leave quick enough. He was caught by the Religious Police having a coffee with a female colleague. They had to show their documents and when they realised the girl was not his wife or sister she was deported back to the States the next day with 'prostitute' stamped on her passport."

"Do they have religious police in Oman?"

No, but I had to dig out my marriage license and have it validated by a Justice of the Peace before sending the original document to Oman. Philippe suggested I ignore the thing about sending my qualifications to the Oman Embassy in Japan. "You might never see them again," he wrote. "If I were you I'd just take them to your own Education Department and ask them to put half a dozen big fancy stamps on them."

It was hard to think about leaving Sam and Olivia for a whole year. Although they were both married now and settled in their jobs they might not stay in New Zealand all their lives. And what if something happened to them? As if my presence could keep them safe.

"You know what Beth would say, don't you?" Sam and Olivia argued.

"What?"

"GO! GO! GO!"

The quick and the dead

A poster at the intersection warned: *You're a long time dead. So what's the hurry?* Last week it was: *The Quick ARE the Dead.*

The windscreen wipers squeaked and scraped across the mud-spattered glass. I drummed my fingers on the dashboard in time to the rhythm while I waited for the lights to turn green. Why had Norm chosen this morning of all mornings to move his cows? You could never get the muck off the car, even with scrubbing. Not that there'd be any point in saying that to him, of course. He'd only repeat that he'd been moving his cows along that road for a helluva lot more bloody years than the bloody townies had been living in the bloody village and if they didn't bloody like it, tough titties. Apart from the mess on my car he'd also added twenty minutes to my journey, and by the time I arrived in town and driven onto the ring road it was choked with everybody and their grannies. No way was I going to get to class on time. Pity I'd given my students such a bollocking about punctuality yesterday. Oh well.

People were scurrying along the pavement, heads bowed under black umbrellas not designed to ward off freezing horizontal sleet. The trees were bent to the earth, saturated, and leached of colour. I stared at the lights. Still on red. The only spot of colour in this godforsaken morning. The earth was so hard after the nor-westers that the rain was just running off the surface and streaming down the gutters in torrents.

If the rain didn't let up by the time I drove home this afternoon all the fords would be flooded, same as last year.

No.

Not the same as last year.

Nothing was the same as last year.

Last year Beth rode her horse across the flooded ford.

"*It was so deep he had to swim. It was soooo cool. All the trucks were waiting to see how far up his legs the water came.*"

"*It was dangerous! There could have been rusty bed springs, possum traps. You could have drowned.*"

"*Not me.*"

Don't go there. Not before class. Focus on the rain, the people, the car in front.

The young woman in the pale blue Mazda was applying her lipstick in the rearview mirror. How come people didn't get up in time to do all that before leaving for work? Some school children in the bus in front of the Mazda had their faces pressed up against the back window sticking their tongues out at the woman, who was oblivious to their rudeness. I switched the radio on to catch the news. Afghans were throwing bombs at American soldiers, but President Bush reassured the American People and the Free World that he was closing in on Bin

Laden. Someone said something about approaching the first anniversary of September 11.

I fumbled for the switch.

September 11, 2001. Lying in bed reading. Wriggling my toes into the softness of the new sheepskin underlay. Beth padding down the hall and opening her door. Holding out the finished oil pastel of Jack. Grinning: "*I couldn't wait till tomorrow to show you so Happy Birthday now!*"

"*Oh sweetheart! It's beautiful. You've caught the sunlight in his mane. And the gold of his body. Even the cheeky glint in his eyes. You're so clever!*"

"*So d'ya like it?*"

"*I love it. At the weekend we'll go into town and get a frame.*"

Next morning, Rob's head round the shower door: "*She's in a lot of pain. Says it started when she went to bed last night. We'd better take her straight to the hospital.*"

In the hospital people muttered about planes and towers exploding in New York. In the waiting room the TV screen showed people jumping from windows.

The oncologist wiped his forehead with the back of his arm: "*So at least we now know the tumour originated in the appendix. Extremely rare. Almost unheard of in this age group. In effect the appendix exploded. We'll try chemotherapy. However ...*"

The lights turned green. Focus on the lights. The bus full of children. The lipstick lady. The man in the van in the next lane picking his nose. Do people in cars think they're invisible? WE'RE WELL HUNG!! the writing on the side of the van proclaimed. Window frames. Door frames.

What was wrong with this traffic? Probably roadworks further up. Turn the radio back on. Must be some music on somewhere. "... *so if Bush thinks that blasting a few Al Qaeda cells will eliminate terrorism he is very much mistaken. For every cell destroyed, hundreds more will grow and spread* ...”

Oh, for God's sake get a move on! How many times does this bloody light have to turn green before anybody bloody moves? Has the whole bloody world gone into slow motion?

The bus slowly drifted forward. The woman in the blue Mazda didn't notice the lights had changed again and was putting the finishing touches to her eyeliner. I tapped the horn to encourage the car in front to move off. Before it did so the bus gathered speed, only to jam on its brakes as the truck in front hadn't noticed the changing lights. On the back of the bus there was a large poster advertising the ice rink and as the bus moved away a picture of an ice hockey goalie, a speed skater and a figure skater came into view. I couldn't make out the words beneath. My heart banged against my ribcage.

Last winter Beth had persuaded me to watch an ice hockey game against the Canadian Wildcats. "*You can't not come Mum! It's an honour for me to be selected for the National Team!*"

At the ice rink I'd shivered, even though I had a blanket and a hot water bottle on my knee:

"*What if she gets hurt?*"

Rob: "*Then she'll know how to avoid getting hurt the next time.*"

The president of the trekking club: "*You should have seen her, Alexa! Hair flowing in the wind. Galloping up the hill bareback on Bob.*"

The phone call from Charlie: "*Is she home yet?*"

"*No. What's happened now? Did the horse throw her again?*"

"*Not this time. No, she's got the young bugger goin' good. She offered to help with the shearin'. Tried to tackle a ram and he jumped up and whacked her in the mouth. The teeth are still attached, but she'd better see the dentist.*"

And on the way to the dentist: "*Mum, you're doing 120k! Calm down will ya!*"

In the dental surgery one of the men in paint-stained overalls put down his roller and said, "*The surgery's closed for paintin' but seein' as you're here I'll have a look meself. Hop into the chair.*" And at the expression on Beth's face, "*Just jokin' ha ha. I AM the dentist. No, truly!*"

We'd been living in the village just a few months. After our year in Brazil, Beth had wanted to live in the country so she could look out of her bedroom window and see her horses. "*And I want to go to uni to do farm management.*" And then one day: "*I told Charlie I don't want to be a farmer after all. Going up and down in that* tractor all day – oh man! I've decided to go to Art School instead. I've joined a drama group. They told us there are calls for people with horses to go and audition for the Black Riders in Lord of the Rings. Thought I might give that a go."

"Fine. Art School's a better choice. Farming's too dangerous. By the way, when did your hair turn green? The last time I looked it was pink."

"Green is the colour for Rowan, the tree spirit."

When the phone rang and the voices on the other end asked for Rowan, Rohanna, Brigitte, Morgan or Ewlin, I learned not to say "wrong number".

"People change their jobs, their cars, their clothes. I think it's kinda cool changing my name to suit the occasion."

"I took Bob out for a ride last night. There was no moon. Everything was pitch black. I stretched my arms out like wings and closed my eyes and put him into a slow canter. It was fantastic. Like flying."

"It was dangerous. You could have been killed."

"Not me."

"How many lives do you think you have?"

"Nine. Like my cat."

At Art School Beth sketched an oil pastel of her Siamese cat. The blue eyes blazing. The claws poised to draw blood. In the gleaming round black pupils there was a reflection of a tiny mouse sitting back on its haunches, hands on hips, mocking the idea of death.

The bus gathered speed again.

The lipstick lady fluffed out her hair and turned left.

The well hung van man stopped drilling his nose and turned right.

The bold black letters of the ice rink advertisement reared up under the three skaters:

GO HARD! GO FAST! GO FIGURE!
GO! GO! GO!

The skin that separates water and air

Melanie touched the small leather pouch on the chain around her neck and fingered the contents, thinking of Vincent's first tactic which had been to say Bruce was a good man and didn't deserve to go down when he'd already apologised. When that didn't work he'd said the publicity would embarrass her kids.

"And your mum's talkin' crap when she says I'm only worried about the stuff on my camera comin' out. There's no jury in the world would think there's anything wrong in controlled lovin' situations."

Melanie slackened the reins on Bob's neck and let him go at his own pace. He picked his way carefully over the rough river stones, trampling crowds of Californian poppies thrusting their faces at the pale sun. Their stoicism amazed her. Every winter the river flooded, wiping out all vegetation and turning the river bed into a bleak expanse of bare grey gravel. Then back came the spring and back came the flowers.

She slid off Bob's back and opened the gate. As she led him through, she stroked the soft hairs around his nostrils. Until she'd seen Beth's oil pastel sketch of him she'd never noticed the hairs that grow on horses' nostrils. He waited patiently while she closed the gate and hopped on his back again. She paused before leaning slightly forward to signal he could go, the way Beth had taught her, the conversation with Beth still playing word-for-word in her head.

"Never dig your heels into a horse's sides to get him to move off. Just think how you'd feel if someone poked you in the ribs instead of asking you politely to walk forward."

She'd told Beth she did know how that felt and that's why she wanted to leave Vincent.

"But you've just got married!"

"Yeah."

"So …?"

"Hard to figure out, eh? He said he could help me detox."

"And did he?"

"Yeah. He let me stay in the camping ground in the old gypsy caravan he was renovating. Put rose petals in the bush bath he'd rigged up. Let me sleep as long as I wanted. Encouraged me to help him paint the caravan. Red and gold. I loved doing that. Then he let me do the bookings and look after his old Clydesdale. He couldn't believe I'd grown up in the country and never had my own horse."

She'd known about all the women and tried not to feel jealous when she saw the photographs in the caravan, but it was hard not to mind when they rang him at all hours of the day and night. He'd had trespass orders put on three of them. The last one was because the ex had broken in and hidden in a cupboard when he brought another woman home and had sprung out like a demented cat and ripped into the pair of them with her fingernails. At the wedding some of the camp residents whispered that they hoped for a bit of peace and quiet now. "We were getting sick of the Police coming round all the time," they said.

"*What a thing to say at my wedding, eh?*"

Beth laughed so hard she nearly fell off the horse.

She'd tried to stay up late when he threw the first party, but four o'clock in the morning was way later than she was used to. Vincent woke her up blazing at her "rudeness". That was the first time he'd locked her out of the caravan.

That was the first time he'd locked her out of the caravan.

"*So that's why you were walking down the street at 7am?*"

"*Yeah. He'd taken the keys of the car and I thought I could walk to the bus stop and get a bus into town.*"

"*You could've got in the car with Mum and me.*"

She was too embarrassed. How can you say you're leaving when you've only been married a week? "*Anyway, he caught up with me and I got in his car. He was pretty good about it really. All I had to do was apologise and he was okay.*"

Beth had stared at her.

"*YOU had to apologise? JEEZ!*"

That was all very well for her to say. Back then Beth's life had been full of horses and Art School. She'd inhabited a perfect world until tests showed what the pain in her belly was. Even then Beth shrugged it off saying she was treating it like flu. *"I just can't stand the way that doctor puts his head in his hands every time he sees me."*

Vincent didn't mind her going to see Beth, as long as she didn't stay away too long. He'd even encouraged her to go riding with Beth. *"It'll do you good, Melanie,"* he'd said. *"Good for both of you."* He sometimes came with her to visit Beth and to bring her incense and candles, and sometimes special oils she could put in her bath. When he found Alexa, Beth's mum, crying in the paddock one day he wrapped her up in a green cashmere shawl that had belonged to his own mother.

A few weeks after Beth died Melanie took her mum, Noeline, over to have a cup of tea with Alexa and Alexa showed them the shawl. She said it was one of the kindest things anyone had ever done for her. Noeline responded that she was just waiting for the opportunity to push Vincent down the stairs. Or into the bush bath. Alexa's eyes widened so then Noeline had to try and set her straight and tell her about the knicker fetish.

Vincent had already explained it was just a guy thing, but Melanie saw Alexa's eyebrows shoot into her hairline as Noeline went on about the pile of mags she'd found and hidden in one of the sheds so the children wouldn't see them. Even though all guys, as Vincent explained, read that stuff, you didn't have to go telling people, but once Noeline got going it would've been easier to stop a train. So then out came the story about when she'd wandered into the camp kitchen to make a cup of tea and saw what he was watching on the computer and how Vincent had laughed and said she was lucky she hadn't caught him playing with his crown jewels. Melanie cringed and shrank as each story came out, but Alexa didn't say a word.

A few days later they were sitting on the paddock gate watching the horses graze and Alexa started talking about the first time they'd met Vincent when he'd helped them catch Beth's horse that had run off and ended up in the camping ground.

"I thought he was a bit eccentric," she said, "butterflies tattooed all over his head. But harmless and kind. And that gypsy caravan! A work of art! He told me his dream was to get it to a state where he could lease it out to people for holidays, so they could slow down and appreciate the landscape, instead of seeing it speed by from inside a goldfish bowl. And those paintings he did of wildflowers!"

All Melanie could do was nod.

She thought of the night Vincent had found the remains of sleeping pills at the bottom of his Milo and the way he had stared at her. Melanie told him they were to help her sleep and she must have mixed up the cups. His eyes narrowed, but he didn't say anything. The doctor advised her to have some counselling, but when she made the appointment Vincent insisted on going too, and she couldn't describe how dirty she felt inside. When they left he told her all counsellors were wankers.

★

Bob spotted the waterhole at the end of the track and let out a long sigh. Melanie slid off his back, loosened his bridle and saddle and pulled her juice bottle from the saddle bag.

"*I'm never going to get married,*" *Beth had said when they stopped at the waterhole.* "*Guys just slow you down. I've got too much stuff to do.*"

"*So what about Darryn and Nathan then? They're around often enough.*"

"*Nah!*" *Beth laughed.* "*They're my best mates. They bought an old car and keep it in one of our paddocks. We spray-painted it red and yellow and orange!*"

"*Yeah, I saw you all hooning along the riverbed one day. Looked like fun.*"

Beth glanced at her.

"*Reckon you don't get much of that, eh? Does your mum help out with the kids?*"

"*She spoils them rotten. Especially Lisa because she looks like my brother Peri who died soon after I was born.*"

"*How'd he die?*"

"*Leukaemia.*"

Beth picked up a pine cone and threw it into the river, breaking up the reflected sky.

"*How'd your mum cope with that?*"

"*Her milk dried up. She said she'd asked God to take me instead.*"

Beth lay down on her stomach and looked into the river. Melanie flopped down beside her. Two faces stared back, as if they were under water, looking up.

"Must've made you feel real wanted, eh?" said Beth.

Melanie didn't answer.

Beth flicked at the water with her fingers.

Two weeks after Beth died Melanie stood in the paddock with Vincent talking to Beth's parents. Beth's dad, Rob, climbed onto Molly's bare back, the way Beth used to, even though he didn't know the first thing about horses. Just as Melanie was thinking she'd better fetch a bridle, Molly ran off. Rob slipped over her neck and fell to the ground. Alexa stood like a statue. Rob's eyeballs rolled up into his head and he passed out. Vincent pushed him over on his side then ran into the house to call the ambulance. Melanie went with them to the hospital to give the ambos the information they needed because they couldn't get any sense out of Alexa. Every time Rob came to he said, "She's dead, isn't she? She's dead!" then passed out again. And Alexa just rocked back and forth, clawing at her face.

It turned out Rob only had concussion. By the time they got back home late that night Vincent had cooked a meal and left it in their oven, and lit a fire. So how in the world did it get from there to where he threatened to put broken glass in the horses' feed?

It wasn't that Vincent was violent. It was just the way he kept waking her up to explain what she needed to do to get her act together and make the marriage work that did her head in. He always had heaps more words than she could cope with. She used to make Beth laugh telling her some of the things he said and saying them out loud made them feel not so bad.

She'd liked bringing over little things for Beth each day – a picture she'd made with a four-leafed clover, a lavender pillow to help her sleep, stuff like that. After Beth died Vincent wasn't so tolerant if she stayed with Alexa too long. One day he showed her the log he'd been keeping of all the times she'd gone over there and how many hours and minutes she'd spent. It was true, it did all add up to quite a bit of time, though as she'd tried explaining, it wasn't as if she had any other friends, but Vincent said it ate into their quality time.

Quality time. Yeah, well. Still, to be fair, it was true when he said she'd had no right to go and tell Alexa about him filming the business with that hitchhiker. But with Beth gone, and no one to tell, things kind of built up. And she shouldn't have told him what Alexa said about the hitchhiker thing. He forbade her to see Alexa after that, but she managed to sneak out one day when he was up at the pub.

They'd sat in Alexa's sunroom and the rain was streaking past the windows in solid diagonal stripes. Thunder rattled the sky and lightning shredded it to zigzags of green, pink and blue. If it hadn't been so scary it would have been beautiful. And on the wall there was that photo of Beth with her arm around Leonardo, the boy she'd met in Brazil six years ago when she was seventeen. He'd come over to New Zealand three times, to see her. The first time for a month's holiday, and a couple of years later to work. That was when she'd heard him crying behind the old grey poplar in Alexa's garden. Beth told her they'd split up. It was real sad because she'd also heard him singing Italian opera behind that tree, with nobody to appreciate it but the sheep.

She told Beth most girls would kill to have someone as hot as that and Beth said well probably, but she wasn't most girls. Even so she painted a picture of the tree and had it printed on a T-shirt to send him for his birthday and told him it was so he could wear the tree next to his heart.

The third time he came back was a month before Beth died. When Alexa had finally stopped taking her to that weird light therapy clinic in Auckland. When Beth refused to take any more homeopathy, acupuncture and carrot juice. When her best friend came back from Australia. When Beth asked her brother and sister to sleep a couple of nights in the garden with her, like when they were kids. Leonardo came back. He baked some special cheese bread and they played music in the garden all night with Beth wrapped up in quilts, and Vincent fed wood into the brazier, and Rob lit sparklers to add a bit of magic.

And there she was in the photo. Her long tanned legs, blonde hair and wide grin. As if all her plans for the future were going to happen. As if she had all the time in the world. And maybe it was the rain or the photo, but something in Melanie's heart broke. Like when the stop bank disintegrated in last winter's flood, laying bare years of buried rubbish that was tossed about in the river, forcing new routes through the sludge for the snow–melt off the mountains in spring.

Alexa listened. And gave Melanie the name of a lawyer. And a book to read. "Hide it where Vincent won't find it."

But Vincent did find it. And that's when he said the thing about feeding glass to the horses. And to Alexa he wrote a note. In the morning when he went to pick up his mail he found his mother's green shawl wrapped up in tissue paper in the mailbox. "She didn't have to do that," he said, wiping tears from his eyes.

That night Melanie swallowed a handful of sleeping pills, and that's why, when Vincent sent Bruce up to their bedroom, to "talk some sense into her" she was too dozy to push him out the door.

She'd almost fallen down the stairs on her flight to the phone, but she was able to dial the police before Bruce burst through the doorway calling her a liar and Vincent said when the police found out she'd worked on Manchester Street they'd just laugh at her. But the police didn't laugh. They did, however, search the house, and take away Vincent's camera.

She told the policewoman she couldn't understand why it had got to her so much because, as Vincent kept saying, the first time would surely have been the worst considering she'd only been nine, but she'd handled it real well back then and just blotted it out of her mind so why couldn't she now?

And the policewoman raised one eyebrow and said, "Real well Melanie, eh?"

Last week the policeman brought the camera back. He warned Vincent it didn't look good and the Prosecution would make a meal of it. And Vincent said that was crap because it was a controlled loving situation, not like Angelo's Angels, eh? And by the way what did Melanie think Alexa would say if she knew about Angelo's Angels? And she didn't bother telling him Alexa already knew.

It was so peaceful here by the river, the sky and clouds and trees mirrored on its glassy surface.

"A perfect upside-down world," she'd said to Beth.

"Nah!" Beth threw a stone into the middle of the river and broke the reflection. "It's not real."

"Well, what IS real?"

Bob snorted, munched and farted.

"That's real," grinned Beth.

And they'd laughed till their stomachs hurt. Till the tears rained down their cheeks. As if it was the funniest thing they'd ever heard.

Last night Melanie had dreamed of Beth. They were floating under water, here in the river, with their faces turned to the sky. When she woke up her face was wet.

And this morning she went to the butcher's and on the back wall there was a wooden panel she couldn't remember seeing before with words burned into it and she started to read them aloud. "The air is torn and thundering, skimming the earth …"

She stopped and stared and the butcher finished the line for her, thinking she couldn't see it properly, "Everything turns to wind and everything on earth comes flying past."

He slapped her packet of mince on the counter. "The bloke that made it said it comes from a joker called Gogol. Whoever he is he musta been here in a nor'wester, eh?"

And the only thing that made any sense was that she needed to ride by the river again.

And so here she was. Taking the pouch off the chain around her neck. Shaking her wedding ring onto her palm. Drawing back her arm. The ring flying through the air in a perfect arc. Glistening in the sun. Landing in the river. The thin skin on the surface of the water split into shards like shattered glass. Like a broken reflection. Like a fragment of something real.

When the wind died

The winds blew in off the Tasman, climbed and descended the Southern Alps and blasted across the Canterbury Plains. Such ferocity was unmatched since records began, according to meteorologists, fuelling concerns about a climate shift. Not so, said Zekkie Bean, who ran the village pub. Fifty years ago she blew a good'un, uprooted trees, lifted roofs, raked the earth and sucked moisture out of river stones. Part of a cycle, he said. That was no comfort to drought-weary farmers shifting dead sheep from the parched rivers each day, while wind-fanned grass fires consumed the pastures. The District Council warned people to turn off garden hoses and limit their showers. Those dependent on rainwater were already buying in tanker loads from town.

Melvin Huffer finished testing the water level in the Shellharts' well and carried his instruments over to his van, bracing his head against the wind. It sounded like a stampede of wild horses shredding the air with their hooves. No wonder the Shellharts' Dalmation was barking fit to burst. He watched it leaping about on the end of its chain, and in the same moment saw the top branch of a hundred-year-old Norfolk pine twist like a corkscrew, suspend itself in mid-air for an instant, then crash to the ground, shaving branches off the pin oak and golden elm. It landed less than a metre away from the dog, across what had been, a minute earlier, Deidre and Daniel Shellhart's prize-winning rose garden.

"Bugger!" Melvin muttered, and for the first time in thirty years made the sign of the cross. The dog whined and crawled back into its kennel. Melvin climbed into his van and scribbled a note for the Shellharts suggesting they give him a tinkle if they wanted that tree sawn up. Bit of extra money for Gideon, he reckoned. God knows he'd need it now, flaming idiot. Melvyn sighed and shoved the note in the mailbox on his way out. As he drove to the pub he realised his nose was bleeding for the third time in two days.

Over tea that evening Dinah told him that in the days before roads connected Woolbedding to Christchurch, the pine trees owned by Catholic families had been pruned of their highest branches, leaving a tall bare trunk with a pom-pom of foliage at the top to make it visible to the Catholic priest doing his Sunday rounds in his pony and trap.

"I read that somewhere when we were gathering information for the school centennial," she said, spooning silverbeet onto Melvin's plate and adding another dollop to Gideon's. "Well, that's another bit of history vanished. Deidre'll be so upset."

"She'd be a helluva lot more upset if it had landed on her roof," said Melvin.

"That's why you crossed yourself," said Dinah, "out of gratitude that it didn't."

"Dunno. Not that I believe in omens and stuff like that," Melvin shrugged. "But when I saw the way that thing twisted and fell ... bloody weird."

"That's the *Foehn* effect," said Dinah. "On that documentary on climate shift the other night somebody said the wind is called a *Foehn*, like the wind that blows down from the Swiss Alps. He said there are more migraines, depressions and suicides, more crimes committed when a *Foehn* blows. Seven out of ten people have a reaction. It's all to do with positive ions in the air affecting mood. He said a feeling of foreboding is very common. Deidre told me that in some parts of the world people call them Witch's Winds."

"Yeah, well," said Melvin, and reached for more gravy. He turned to his son who was staring morosely at the food on his plate. "When I called in at the pub Zekkie told me Alexa and Rob are moving to the Middle East for a year."

Dinah looked up, "Oh? So they've made up their minds then? Good on them! A change like that could be just what they need."

"Yeah," agreed Melvin. "Losing a beaut kid like Beth. Makes no sense. I'll never forget that time last spring when the ford was flooded. The rain hosing down and me wondering if I could risk the truck. I look up and there's Beth riding her horse bareback across the ford, big bloody grin on her face, waving her hand at me, soaked to the skin and having the time of her life."

Gideon pushed his chair away and stood up.

"Anyway, what I was getting at," continued Melvyn, "was that they want someone to look after their house for the year. They don't want any rent, in exchange for taking care of the garden, feeding the chooks, the goat, the cats and the dog. The horses are going somewhere else. Could be just the ticket for you and Melanie. A whole year. Give the pair of you a chance to get on your feet."

Gideon strode towards the door. "Nah. It's all off. Me and Mel split up."

His parents froze with their forks halfway to their mouths.

"Split up? But what about the ...?" Dinah began.

Gideon's hand was on the door handle. "It's sorted."

"Sorted?"

Gideon slammed the front door behind him.

"Leave him be," said Melvin. "How could we be 100% certain it was his anyway?"

"But ..."

"Vincent's back. And we all know what that means."

Melanie put the blue box back in the fridge and stood there for a moment, breathing in the cold air. She closed the door and wiped the sweat off her brow with the hem of her T-shirt.

"Mum, I saw Alexa about the house this morning. She doesn't want any rent, just the animals and garden taken care of. It'd get me and Katie and Lisa out of your hair."

Noeline finished spooning chopped banana into Katie's mouth. "Up to you, doll. You know you're welcome to stay here as long as you want."

"I know, but it's time for me to move on now. New start."

Noeline lifted the child out of the high chair. "I'll put her to bed. There's fresh lemonade in the fridge. Pour us some, eh?"

Melanie opened the fridge again. The jug of lemonade stood behind the blue box. Lisa tugged at her shorts. "Mummy, can I see the bub again?"

"No, sweetpea."

"Why?"

Melanie closed the fridge door. "Coffee'll do."

She flicked a teaspoon of instant into two mugs and returned to the fridge to get the milk. As soon as her fingers touched the handle they flew off it as if it were hot. "Black'll be fine." She poured boiling water into the mugs and carried them over to the table. Lisa climbed onto her knee.

Noeline padded back into the kitchen and flopped into the chair. "She went straight off, wee lamb." She stared at the coffee in the mug in front of her. "I done all that lemonade – waddya make black coffee for?" She caught the expression on Melanie's face and fumbled for her cigarettes in her jeans pocket. "Oh, doll, I'm sorry. It's this damn wind. Your nanna used to call it an ill wind. An ill wind blows nobody no good, that's what she used to say."

Melanie sat very still.

Noeline lit her cigarette and inhaled deeply. "I have to speak my mind about what you done. Gideon's a good bloke. Not like Vincent."

"It wouldn't have worked," said Melanie. "And it has nothing to do with Vincent coming back."

Noeline blew the smoke out very slowly. "When I was cleaning Shellhart's the other day Deidre said people shouldn't make decisions when a Witch's Wind blows. Something to do with electrical thingies in the air that do your head in so you can't think straight."

"Too late now," said Melanie.

"What's a Witch's Wind?" piped Lisa.

"Nan's too tired to explain, darlin'." Noeline stubbed her cigarette out. "Well, what's done's done. So where the hell has Andy got to? How long does it take to find a stone in the river, for God's sake? The flamin' river's full of them. We may as well go down the pub for a bit. I need something to calm my nerves before we … before …"

Melanie stirred. "I've found a good spot, Mum. Under the old macrocarpa. D'you remember the swing Dad made for me there with ropes and an old tyre? No matter how hard he pushed me I'd scream, "Higher, higher!" my head tipped right back, my ears full of the sound of baby pigeons, butterflies swooshing in my belly, the wind on my face, higher, higher, till I was flying in the sky. And Dad, standing there, solid as a tree, feet planted like roots, ready to catch me if I fell."

"There won't be any left," said Noeline, gulping a

mouthful of coffee. "Baby pigeons. They'll all've been blown out of their nests in this wind."

Melanie kissed the top of Lisa's head. "I'm naming him Peter. After my Dad."

"Like Peter Rabbit?" said Lisa. She wriggled off her mother's knee and ran to her room.

Noeline dropped her mug on her lap and yelped as the hot liquid soaked through her jeans. She jumped up and grabbed a tea towel from the bench. "Oh for God's sake! Look I'm going down the pub. Come on, Mel."

"We can't leave the kids, Mum!"

"Andy'll be here soon. It'll be okay."

Lisa ran back into the room holding a threadbare rabbit by its one remaining ear. She danced it in the air. "Susie Rabbit Peter Rabbit Susie Rabbit Peter Rabbit."

"Oh, Jesus Mary and Joseph!" Noeline gasped. She tore her jeans and t-shirt off and threw them on the back of the chair. "Lisa babe, you won't mind if me and Mummy go out for a bit?"

Lisa shook her head.

Noeline disappeared into her bedroom and immediately returned pulling a clean dress over her arms.

Melanie didn't move. "We haven't got any money for the pub."

"Andy put twenty dollars in Lisa's piggybank when he had that win," said Noeline, yanking a brush through her hair. "You don't mind if we borrow it, do you Lis?"

Lisa shook her head.

Noeline rattled some coins out of the china pig.

Melanie sighed and kissed the child's cheek. "Stay in the chair and have a wee sleep till Andy gets back. Don't open the door to nobody."

The front door banged shut. Lisa stared at it then climbed into the armchair. The wind rattled the window frames and scraped the trees against the glass. It hooted down the chimney of the old potbelly stove and whispered through cracks in the walls and the old wooden floor. Lisa drew deeper into the worn vinyl of the chair and leaned against Noeline's T-shirt, her rabbit cradled tight against her chest. "Peter Rabbit Peter Rabbit Peter Rabbit," she crooned, till she fell asleep.

The knock was so loud Lisa jumped, sending her rabbit skittering across the floor. She slithered out of the chair, scooped the rabbit up by the leg and ran across the room to open the door. Andy must've forgotten his key again. But it was Mrs Shellhart standing there, holding a blue box.

"Hello, Lisa dear. Is Mummy or Nan in? I'm collecting for Plunket."

Lisa put her head on one side and considered. They said not to let nobody in, but Mrs Shellhart wasn't nobody. She was somebody. She'd heard Andy say so.

"Bitch thinks she's somebody," Lisa said.

Mrs Shellhart blinked at her.

Katie started wailing. Mrs Shellhart peered into the lounge. "Where's Mummy, sweetheart?"

"Down the pub," said Lisa.

Mrs Shellhart took a deep breath, looked at her watch, strode past Lisa and followed the wailing to the bedroom. She plucked Katie out of her cot and wrinkled her nose. "Show me where the nappies are, love."

Lisa opened the cupboard door, stood on tiptoe, and pulled a packet of disposables from the shelf. Mrs Shellhart put a clean one on Katie, carried her back into the kitchen, deposited the dirty nappy in the bin and washed her hands at the kitchen sink, holding Katie against her hip. She looked at her watch again. She couldn't just walk out and leave these two mites here all alone. It was completely beyond her, she'd only been saying to her sister on the phone the other night, why it was always the ones who couldn't give a fig who could breed like rabbits, while people like her would have given ten, no, twenty, years of her life to have just one, and would even have adopted if there'd been any left to adopt. It was all very well for her sister, with her five boys, to say blood will out. Who could not love these two wee moppets here and if one started thinking about *their* blood … yes, well, who said life was fair? She glanced at her watch again. She had to get back before Gideon finished sawing up that fallen branch so she could ask him to stack it in the woodshed, otherwise Daniel would insist on doing it himself and he was already so upset about the roses and what with his heart and everything … she could wait a few minutes, but that's all, then she'd just have to take the children home with her and leave Melanie a note. And quite honestly, she wasn't sure if Child Welfare shouldn't be involved. She'd have to see what Daniel thought. She settled herself in the chair in the lounge with the toddler on her lap. She rattled the coins in the Plunket box at Katie, who beamed and banged it with her fat little fist.

Lisa stood in front of her, staring at the box. "Is that box for babies?"

"That's right, dear. I've been collecting all morning."

Lisa sucked her rabbit's ear. "How many babies you got in there?"

"Oh no no no no, sweetheart! I've only got *money* in here. *Money* for the babies!"

Lisa frowned at the box, not entirely convinced. She wanted to look inside, just to be sure, but Mrs Shellhart was speaking again.

"That's a lovely little bunny, dear. What's his name?"

"It's a her," said Lisa.

"Oh? She's a little girl bunny, is she? What's she called?"

"Susie," said Lisa.

"Susie? That's a very pretty name. When I was a little girl I had a rabbit called Peter. A real rabbit. I kept him in a little cage in the garden shed."

Lisa rubbed Susie's ear against her cheek. "We have a Peter, too."

Mrs Shellhart's smile broadened. "Have you indeed? Well fancy that! And where *is* Peter darling?"

Lisa traced round Susie's worn face with the tip of her finger. "In the fridge."

Mrs Shellhart chuckled. "That's a good idea, in this hot weather. Keep him nice and cool."

Lisa stared at Mrs Shellhart, the Plunket box, the fridge, then back at Mrs Shellhart. "Do you want to see him?"

Mrs Shellhart breathed in the talcum powdery scent of Katie's hair. "I'd love to see him pet." Though she said so herself she did have a way with little ones.

Lisa skipped into the kitchen. She opened the fridge door and took out the blue box.

Andy left Frosty on the passenger seat in case he started barking. He walked round to the back of the truck and heaved the stone off. He hoped they hadn't heard him pulling into the paddock. He wanted to get everything ready first, then go and tell them. Get it all over and done, quick smart. This stone was some weight all right, but it would stop the dog diggin'. Bad enough when the cat dragged that newborn rabbit in last night. Pity Noeline saw it before he'd had time to scrape it off the floor. It wouldn't be a bad idea to nail the cat flap up. The cats wouldn't be too rapt, but still, just for a bit. Anyway, he was pleased with this stone. A real nice blue. He'd never seen one shaped like a heart before, neither. It was well worth the search. Mel would be stoked. He carried it over to the base of the macrocarpa and laid it on the ground.

Nice sheltered spot here, out of that damned nor'wester. Better grab the spade and get the hole dug.

The joker on the telly the other night said the wind had a heap of names. Chinnook, the American Indians called it. And what was the name of that song? *They call … the wind … Marie? … Maria?* Whatever. It'd been like trying to work in a flamin' dragon's mouth these last seven days.

Andy straightened up slowly and rubbed the bottom of his back with his knuckles. All the jelly had dried out of his bones. Noeline was always on at him to get an x-ray, but once they got you in hospital they found all sorts of things wrong with you. Andy stepped back and looked at the hole. Just a bit deeper.

Fuck knows what the hospital was thinkin' of. Some flamin' social worker's idea of a Good Thing. Yeah, right! The expression on Noeline's face when she looked in that box … oh man! In bed last night, her tears soaking the hairs on his chest. He took his hanky out of his pocket and wiped his face. He inhaled and exhaled loudly, just to hear the air moving in and out of his lungs. The sooner Mel got her own place the better. He could help out a bit with the rent. And that little snot, Gideon whatsihisface should be made to cough up. Better not say anything to Noeline though. Not just yet. She had enough on her plate. He dug out the last spadeful of earth and surveyed his handiwork. Maybe a few flowers? It would look a bit bare with just the stone. He peered over the fence at the borders of shrivelled marigolds. Right. Just the stone then. He took out his hanky to polish it up a bit.

As he bent over the blood rushed to his head and he thrust out a hand against the macrocarpa to steady himself.

The rough bark under his spread fingers had bits of fibre sticking out where a rope had long since grown into the trunk and become part of the tree. Something more than his balance had shifted, but he couldn't figure out what. Like the world had suddenly stopped spinning. Then it dawned on him. The wind had died. Funny expression that. He could hear the pigeons hooting like crazy because a nest had been blown clean out of the tree onto the ground. He picked it up and saw a fledgling inside. It was limp and almost transparent, a thin membrane over its bulging eyes. Poor little bugger was still warm. He looked down into the hole. Yeah, why not? He'd tell Melanie. Might make her feel a bit better.

Oman

2003 – 2004

Connecting

11th July

Hi Olivia and Sam,

Here we are in Oman. Finally! Heathrow was a nightmare with roads tangled like spaghetti, frenetic traffic all the way to the airport, and angry people having tantrums at the check-in. At least the trip was fast – only five hours, changing at Dubai and then another hour to Muscat.

In Muscat we had to go into two separate queues. I picked up my work visa just before I went to the passport control. We'd had to stay in England an extra week because Hussein, the 'CEO' hadn't organised my visa in time despite the fact I'd sent all those documents off months ago. I should have listened to my own threat not to leave New Zealand until the visa and the contract were in my hands. Your father had to go to a separate queue for his visitor's visa because Hussein hadn't managed to arrange a permanent one for him in time.

The queues at all the counters were a mile long except for the one your father went to, but we both emerged at the same time. As soon as we left the airport the heat melted our eyeballs. Incredible heat, around 40 degrees, but apparently the hottest time (50 degrees) is over, and the temperature will start to decrease to a pleasant 28 degrees by November. Philippe, the Director of Studies, met us at the airport and took us to our hotel – a tacky, run-down Holiday Inn, in an industrial area. He left us at the hotel to unpack and get sorted out then picked us up a couple of hours later.

Philippe drove us around Muscat to get us orientated to the city. It's on the coast and surrounded by rocky mountains and desert. The roads are immaculately clean (swept by hundreds of Indian workers each day) and lined with native trees, mostly date palms and flame trees which have huge bright red flowers. Minah birds roost in the trees. They are very vociferous birds. Bougainvillea, with hot pink blossom, spreads over fences and walls. Most of the flowers are in hot colours of bright pink, red and orange, interspersed with white jasmine and frangipani.

The whole city has been developed only in the last thirty years and the architecture is stunning – traditional Arabian with arched windows and doors. The material is cement in soft colours – white, cream and sand - which are easy on the eye, nothing harsh or gaudy, and the lines are clean and flowing. The city is well designed and aesthetic.

Philippe took us inside a flash hotel – the Al Bustan Palace Hotel – to look at the mosaics and domed ceiling of the interior. There was an area in the foyer set up like a traditional Arabian living room, with red carpets and cushions on the floor, where an old Omani man in a long white shirt, called a *dishdasha*, and a white turban, was serving dates and coffee. We sat there cross-legged on the cushions while he poured us Omani coffee out of a copper coffee pot into tiny cups. The coffee was flavoured with cardamom, saffron and rosewater. He showed us how to ask for more coffee, by holding out the cup, and how to refuse it by shaking the cup from side to side. After the coffee he sprinkled rose water on our hands.

We stopped at a beach to watch children playing in the water. Some fishermen offered to take us out in their boat, but I'm not keen on rowing-boats in the sea. The women were fully clothed in their black *abayas*, wading up to their knees. We saw the Sultan's palace by the harbour, which is only used for administration now. He lives near the airport, heavily guarded. Apparently, there have been several attempts to assassinate him by supporters of his father who didn't take too kindly to having the old Sultan deposed in 1970. Nor are all his attempts at modernisation welcomed by the more conservative elements. Philippe says all this is fairly widely known, but never talked about openly, or publicised in any way. He said he would lend me a book about the assassination attempts. The book is banned in Oman. He said the newspapers only publish good things about the country and the government.

After our tour around the city we went back to Philippe's apartment for dinner and champagne to cele-brate our arrival. His apartment overlooks a private beach and the Arabian Sea. He lives with his partner, Mike, who teaches English at RAFO, the Royal Airforce of Oman. I was surprised, as homosexuality is on the long list of things strictly forbidden here, but they said there's a way round everything.

12th July

After a twelve-hour sleep we went to the Language School, where I met my class, nine men and two women from the *Diwan* – the Royal Court. They are being sponsored by their employers to have English language lessons, after which they'll be sent to university in Australia for three years. The men are all in their thirties and forties and look very imposing in their long white *dishdashas* and embroidered caps. They look like priests, and the two young women look like nuns, which probably accounts for why I feel a bit nervous around them. A convent upbringing is hard to erase. The students call me Mrs Alexa.

The school used to be the house of one of the four wives of the sheik who has the franchise for the school. The house has been gutted and refurbished and looks airy and light with tiled floors and white walls. There is a computer suite, a self-access centre and a language lab. It is in a swish part of town with huge mansions in the neighbourhood.

In the afternoon we went with Philippe and Hussein to look at the apartment they'd found for us. It's a fifteen minute drive from the school in the business district. This area is very noisy, dirty and choked with traffic, so I'm disappointed about that, especially after seeing where

Philippe lives. And it's right next to a school. The other houses in the neighbourhood look run-down. Most of the European ex-pats live in compounds in Al Qurum, the posh part of the city. I guess it's an indication of where teachers are on the social scale. But at least the apartment building is new and the apartment itself is pleasant with tiled floors, white walls, two bedrooms and two bathrooms, a big kitchen and spacious living room. There were a couple of Indians cleaning it while we looked around.

18th July

The company sends its Indian driver, Ravi, to bring me to and from the school each day. He took us to a household goods shop to buy some basic stuff. We bought sheets, towels, pans and a dinner set which were all quite cheap.

When we move into the apartment, we'll get a phone connection and then get connected to the internet and when we do I'll send you this e-mail. Until then I'll just keep adding bits to it. We can't get the phone until I have my Labour Card and today I had to have a million more photos taken to start the process for that. I also have to have a medical and blood test for the Labour Card. We can't buy a car without the Labour Card either, so I hope it won't be too long in coming. Considering how long it took to get the visa processed I can see I'll have to be checking on Hussein every day to make sure he's got onto it.

So far, my impressions are pretty good. The people we have encountered are (mostly) polite and welcoming. The environment is exotic and beautiful and I think it was a good decision to come here. Your father is looking forward to having an entire year where he can focus on writing his book without interruption, although he's hoping to do a bit of lecturing at Sultan Qaboos University and use their library and facilities. They didn't reply to his inquiries from New Zealand for ages and when they did they were vague, so he's going to go and see them.

20th July

On Thursday and Friday, we borrowed Philippe's car and your father drove for the first time in Oman. He managed very well with driving on the right of the road and only forgot twice and went on the left. His sense of direction is amazing too, so we didn't get lost and he remembered where everything was. I think it'll take me a lot longer to become orientated. We walked around a couple of the shopping centres in Al Qurum, an upmarket area. Evening is the best time to walk as the sun goes down at 7.00pm and the twilight is beautiful, with a navy blue sky, a smoky orange sun, and all the lights in the town twinkling. The business hours here are 7.30am to 1.00pm then a three hour lunch break when everybody goes home to sleep, and then from 4.00pm to 8.00pm. Some shops stay open till after 9.00pm and Carrefour – an enormous new French shopping complex – is open 24 hours a day.

The beaches are lovely – long stretches of clean, golden sand with palm trees growing on the beach and woven palm leaf shelters. The sea looks warm and inviting, but we haven't been in yet. We saw some families swimming, the local women in their *abayas*. I suppose the sun is hot enough to dry their clothes while they stand on the beach, but it would be pretty steamy, I think. We've been told that most ex-pat women go to the private beaches to swim to avoid the ogling local men. There is a large population of Indian workers here and they are not allowed to bring their wives, hence the ogling, I suppose. The Omanis stare too, but they're not quite as obvious.

On Friday we went to the supermarket at Carrefour. It has wide aisles and the floor is tiled and scrupulously clean. All the food and products are wrapped and hygienically presented. In addition, there are all the well-known brands of everything and every sign is in English as well as Arabic. That makes the place very easy to survive in. The supermarket also has a houseware section and we bought an ironing board and bits and pieces. Thursday and Friday are equivalent to Saturday and Sunday, so on Friday most shops are closed, but they open at 1.00pm. It was a good time to shop – nice and quiet, because the Omanis are at the mosques.

Later, when they started appearing at the shopping centre, I was fascinated to see the variation in dress. The women wear lovely gauzy black *abayas* and headscarves. The headscarves are embroidered in metallic threads of different colours. Some girls wear jeans under the *abayas*, some wear traditional long tunics with embroidered leggings. Old women wear the full black veil, sometimes with a face mask covering the nose and mouth. Sometimes a veil hides their face completely. Some girls wear make-up and chew gum. I saw one young couple holding hands, but that is an uncommon sight and they were almost certainly married. The children look so sweet with their huge brown eyes, wide smiles, and tiny *dishdashas*. The men wear mostly white *dishdashas*, but some are lilac, blue or black. Mike said that young rebellious men wear dark-coloured *dishdashas* to make a statement about not conforming.

Muscat is an interesting mix of old and new, which I'm sure you would find absolutely fascinating, Olivia. Even you, Sam, would find nothing to object to in the design and layout of the city. There are traditional markets and the one by the harbour is like Aladdin's cave, bursting with treasures. The ceiling is made of woven palm leaves hung with lanterns and the tiny shops are full of copper, silver and gold, spices, fabrics, rugs, and incense. It's where the locals shop and so it's not touristy. The air is fragrant with frankincense and jasmine. At the other end of the scale there are sophisticated shopping malls with clothes from all over Europe, several shops devoted to gold jewellery, others to perfumes and others to make-up. Muscat has a population not much bigger than Christchurch, but many people obviously have a huge disposable income, judging by the number of very fancy shopping malls.

Buildings are just three or four stories high. Nothing can be high enough to prevent a view of the sea and the mountains. There are mosques everywhere that range from the simple white traditional style to stunningly beautiful with blue and gold domes and minarets. The houses vary from simple white buildings in tiny narrow winding streets to palatial mansions in the newer parts of the city.

The harbour, which they call the *Corniche*, has old white Portuguese-style houses with balconies and latticed windows overlooking the sea. The fishermen bring in their catches to the fish market each morning. The first time I walked through I got walloped in the back by the tail of an enormous fish that was being trundled along in a wheelbarrow.

There are sculptures symbolising various aspects of Omani life on every traffic roundabout. So far I've seen an incense burner, coffee pot and cups, fish, a dhow, and a fort complete with canons, a snail, teapot, books, a clock tower and fountains. These are enormous and landscaped with trees and flowers. As many of the roads aren't named, people tend to give directions using the roundabouts as landmarks: "Turn left at the fish, go straight on till you come to the book, go straight ahead for a kilometre then take a right turn at the teapot."

Some of the rock formations lining the roads into the city are flood-lit at night, or painted, or decorated with mosaics, or turned into artificial waterfalls. The effect, on the whole, is quite aesthetic, though I think you, Sam, might feel they are a bit over-the-top. At night the mosques and buildings are lit up and look like something out of Arabian Nights. In the air there is always the scent of frankincense and jasmine and other fragrances I haven't yet identified.

There are signs everywhere showing a trumpet with a line through it which is a warning to drivers not to honk their horns. They still do, however, and I have to say the driving here is abominable. Drivers ignore speed limits, don't signal when changing lanes, and even mount the pavement to push into a line of traffic. Needless to say the accident rate is high. There's no ambulance system for transporting injured people to hospital, though apparently there is one in the process of being organised. The personnel are in the USA being trained. What happens currently is that people who are injured in car accidents tend to get flung into the back of passing pick-up trucks, so I suppose the death rate is high, too. Most of the cars are new. Apparently, drivers can be fined for having a dirty car, though there is no such thing as a Warrant of Fitness test. So your car can be dangerous, but it must be clean.

22nd July

On Saturday we went to the school early because I was supposed to have my fingerprints taken at the Police Station. However, the Omani official who had to accompany me could not be found, so instead we checked out of the hotel and moved our stuff into the apartment. The company is paying for the apartment and electricity.

The furniture is very basic and sparse – a rock-hard blue and cream sofa and chairs, a coffee table and two small side tables, a dining table and four chairs, an entertainment unit, but as there is no television we use it to store books and things.

The curtains they've given us are old and stained, with torn, frayed linings and bits of material tacked onto the hems to make them fit. The fridge was filthy. We cleaned it and left a two-inch patch of dirt and grease on the top, just to remind us of the state it was in when we got it. There is a small laundry with a washing machine that doesn't spin properly, so all the clothes come out dripping wet. Because the air is so hot, however, everything dries over a clothes rack in a couple of hours. The bed is king size – probably from one of the hotels the Sheik owns and there's a child-size dressing table and two small bedside tables. There is air conditioning in every room, apart from the kitchen, although apparently the company will be ordering another air conditioner for us. There's also a ceiling fan in the living room and bedrooms. It's nice having our own space after being cramped in that tacky hotel, even though we're disappointed with the 'suitable furnished accommodation'.

I thought teaching in the late evenings wouldn't be too much of a problem as I could have a lie-in in the mornings. However, there is a primary school right next to our apartment building and the children line up in the yard and salute the flag at 7.30 each morning, while the National Anthem is blasted out on what sounds like an ancient cracked gramophone record, at eardrum-shattering volume, over the entire neighbourhood. This is followed by half an hour of Koran readings by the school principal and various children. These are shouted into the microphone with enormous energy and zeal and the loudspeakers make sure every word penetrates every brain cell for miles around. I asked Hussein if he could find us another apartment but, with his hand over his heart, he sighed and explained that he has signed up for this one for a whole year and can't get out of the contract. He suggested I ask the Principal of the school to turn down the volume. I looked at him to see if he was joking. No, apparently not.

When I asked him to have the curtains, washing machine and fridge replaced he told me to put the request in writing and he would send it to the Board. I did, but I suspect he filed the letter in the bin.

A couple of mornings of being woken by the National Anthem resulted in us having to plan a strategy to help survive the year. It's easier just to go to work.

24th July

My morning class is a noisy, talkative and charming group, though with no apparent study skills, no sense of punctuality, and ten-minute breaks become forty-minute breaks – which probably accounts for the fact that my five-hour mornings seem like half that. Despite daily warnings, their mobile phones still go off all the time in class and they think nothing of having loud, animated conversations into them and with each other in Arabic, even if I'm in the middle of explaining the finer points of the present perfect.

The administration staff at the school are helpful and cheerful. They are Hussein's secretary, Nagwa, who is an Egyptian, Philippe's secretary – an Indian girl called Sugu, and the Omani receptionist, Houda. Because of the government's policy of Omanisation, every business has to employ at least one Omani in a key position. The problem is the company won't pay to have a properly qualified receptionist, so the school is on its third one since I arrived.

The latest incumbent seems reasonably efficient. The one she replaced was an Omani who was born and raised in Zanzibar, so she spoke only Swahili and therefore could not communicate in either Arabic or English. We didn't know she couldn't speak Arabic until one of my students told me she never answered any of their questions. When we told Hussein he simply said we should teach her English. She used to disappear into the prayer room and fall asleep, leaving either no one at the reception desk, or Deepak, the Indian cleaner, in his overalls, with his damp grey cleaning rag, to which he is permanently attached, slung over his shoulder. We convinced Hussein this was not a good look and the girl was replaced. Deepak brings me jasmine flowers each morning to put on my desk. He speaks about three words of English, three of Arabic, and three of Swahili. He throws them at random into his native

Hindi and has extended conversations with me, not a word of which I can understand.

Last weekend my students invited us to a barbecue on the beach. They had prepared all the food and set out woven mats on the beach. The setting was magical. The sea shush-shushing on the sand, the moon shining on the cliffs, turning them the colour and texture of cinder toffee, the lights of the occasional fishing boat far out to sea, and the all-pervading scent of frankincense, jasmine and frangipani on the evening air. The call to evening prayer echoed across the bay. One of the students, Mohammed, was sitting near me and one of the others remarked, "He is a very bad man, sitting beside a lady." This caused roars of laughter and when I said Mohammed was practising because soon he'd be going to Australia where this was normal social behaviour, there was more hilarity at the very idea of this being normal. Two of the others forced themselves to be brave and came and sat beside me too. I suspect they thought of me as an honorary man. They never bring their wives to social functions as women can't socialise with men who are not part of their families. The two girls in the class didn't come to the barbecue for the same reason. Another student, Mahmoud, said he wanted four wives and when he went to Australia he would marry another one there. When we told him it was illegal, he looked quite crestfallen and said Islam allowed it. We said that wouldn't cut much ice with Australian law.

The next day, one of the students, Said, who is a sheik, took us in his car over the mountains to a little fishing village on the coast. The route was like a moonscape, with the jagged tops of the mountains sharply delineated against the sky. Such desolate stark beauty was almost heart-stopping. I thought of you, Olivia and Sam with Beth, striding along the Milford Track with your backpacks. You'd love this landscape. We passed by date plantations and tiny villages where women in colourful clothes carried large pots and bundles of sticks on their heads, and goats and hens wandered across the roads.

Said, like all the students, comes from a village in the interior. His village is in the desert and he owns racing camels. He is the most liberal of the group and there is one – Ahmed – who is very conservative. When I played a song for a listening activity some of the others were singing along, but Ahmed was stony-faced. At the end he told me he didn't like it because listening to songs was not Islamic. I asked why and he said because it distracted us from the serious business of life, such as reading and studying. One of the others assured him this song was educational, not entertainment. He still didn't look convinced. Later he told me he was not sure about going to university in Australia because one of his friends, who is already there, had told him the girls turn up to class every day in their underwear.

After we got back from the drive, Said took us to the place he currently lives while he is studying in Muscat – he works for an oil company which provides houses within a country club with private beach, swimming pool, restaurants and bars. He took us to a bar for dinner and told us he would arrange for us to go to the Club whenever we wanted. He said his father was the ruling sheik of a tribe in the desert and oil had been discovered on his land, which had made him very rich. He invited us to his hometown and said I could ride his camels. He has fifteen and they all have names.

Early one morning, in the middle of my class, Hussein stuck his head round the door and said I had to go to the Police Station to get my fingerprints taken. The Omani official who had to accompany me had finally been located and was there waiting for me at the Police Station. However, the driver, Ravi, who was going to take me there was busy serving tea to the students and couldn't be prised from his position behind the teapot. This had happened once before and he was an hour late in collecting me for something important. While we were in the hotel he collected me each day to take me to the school and around town to buy the things we needed. The only problem was he often didn't come to collect me for a couple of hours and once he disappeared for five hours in the car, leaving me stranded at the school. On that occasion the secretary, seeing how desperate I looked, dashed out into the middle of the road and flagged down a bus full of Indian workers. I think she knew the driver because he wouldn't take any payment. Two of the occupants gave up their seat for me and the bus continued on its way, ricocheting off the pavements as it hurtled down the road in a cloud of smoke and fifteen minutes later screeched to a halt outside our apartment building.

Philippe was furious with Ravi for refusing to be dislodged from the teapot when I was supposed to go to the Police Station, and told him to ask the receptionist to pour the tea instead, but Ravi was shocked at such an idea. Philippe said he felt like saying, "Give me the bloody teapot and I'll pour it myself!" but he didn't because it wouldn't have made any difference.

Finally, I arrived at the Police Station and the official was patiently waiting. He shook my hand and escorted me inside to the ladies only room. Rob had to wait outside. The official stood quietly by while a woman took my fingerprints. When that was done the official solemnly showed Rob the paper with my fingerprints on. I'm not quite sure why. Rob said, "Doesn't look much like her," but I think the humour was lost in the translation. Anyway, it was the last step in the process to get the **LABOUR CARD**.

After I'd finished teaching, Philippe said one of his friends had told him about a car advert he'd seen, so he rang up the owner of the car who turned out to be one of Philippe's neighbours. He took us to see him. The car is a three-year-old white Daewoo Laganza (Korean), in excellent condition and still has three years left on the warranty. We drove it around and decided it was a good bargain. The asking price was $NZ8,500 and we bought it for $NZ7,900. However, we couldn't complete the purchase until I got my Labour Card. We have to go to the Police Station with the owner of the car and do the transfer of ownership papers then.

In the evening we walked to a shop to buy a mobile phone and were very pleased to have it, but then we discovered that we couldn't have it connected to the system until I had the – yes, you've guessed it – Labour Card. This makes no sense at all, but there it is.

31st July

On Monday, the elusive Labour Card, with all its life-giving properties, finally materialised. Whenever we leave the country, for example to go to Dubai for the weekend, we have to show the card at the airport and when we leave for good we have to be escorted out by a policeman and return the Labour Card to him. After all the fuss about the blood test I noticed that they had the wrong blood group printed on the card, but decided not to bother pointing that out.

To celebrate getting the Labour Card we went to a little fish restaurant in Seeb, which is an old town near Muscat. You select your fish from a counter full of ice, and they cook it for you there and then. While it was cooking we went for a walk along the beach and watched groups of boys playing football and some women power-walking in their *abayas*.

When we came back the fish was ready and we sat at a little table outside the restaurant, which was just a simple basic building. The owner, an Egyptian, brought out a huge fish, salad, fresh bread (flat Arabian bread) and hummus. As the sun went down, the lights of the minarets in the mosques flickered on and the call to prayer undulated on the evening air. A few old men came and sat a little distance away from us and chatted together. There were so many feral cats around and two kittens came up to our table and meowed. They were so little and thin with huge ears. We gave them some fish and they fell asleep under the table. I kept thinking that Beth would have taken them home with her. Do you remember that manic orange kitten she brought home in a box, saying she'd found it at the side of the road? It never dawned on me, until you all told me months later that she'd probably got it from the SPCA and then concocted the story about finding it on the way home.

The meal was delicious and unbelievably cheap. Your father insisted on giving the cook more money than he'd asked for, which caused no end of confusion. I told him that I'd read about his fish being the very best grilled fish in the whole of Muscat, and that he was very famous. He understood enough English to know what I meant and grinned from ear to ear.

More on the internet saga. Getting permission for a landline and internet connection necessitated taking a truckload of documents to the Omantel office, only to be told they weren't adequate because not only did my signature need to be notarised, so did all the documents of the English for Life School, including the CEO's signature. The official wrote a note in Arabic to the CEO (the 'highly efficient' Hussein who couldn't organise his way out of a wet paper bag) telling him exactly what extra documentation he needed to supply. A couple of days later, back I went with all the guff, only this time to a different Omantel office near the apartment. The official glared at the pile of paper and said no this wouldn't do at all, he needed the ORIGINAL documents, not photocopies then he could personally photocopy them on the Omantel photocopier which Madam could see behind him. We got into the car and drove to the first Omantel office, found the official who'd written the note in Arabic, plonked the pile down in front of him and waited with baited breath. He scrutinised them, smiled, signed and stamped them and Madam got permission to have a phone.

The date the phone was due to be installed came and went. Several calls to the office over the next few days met with a calm, "No problem Madam. *Bukrah, Inshallah.*" (Tomorrow, if God wills.) God willed the phone to be installed eventually, but the line doesn't work so we still can't get an internet connection. God is evidently snowed under with other Omantel customers at present. We were told by those who've lived here for years that the only way to get action will be to make an appointment with the Public Relations Officer of the company that owns the school and have him sort it out. However, getting an appointment with him will involve another round of *"Bukrah, Inshallah."* Well, Job's tomb is in the south of Oman and the patience of Job is needed to deal with the bureaucracy here.

Your father came into Oman on a visitor's visa because Hussein hadn't got round to organising our visas on time.

The company applied to get it attached to my visa, but evidently the concept of a woman employee bringing her husband in on her visa was too alien for the immigration department even to have a form for it, so his visa was declined on the basis that "Man can bring wife. Woman cannot bring husband." Hussein assured me it was NO PROBLEM. "When Rob's visa expires, we will send you both to Dubai for the weekend then bring him back on another visitor's visa." However, I suspect nothing will happen until the day the visa expires then there'll be another panic. It seems to be the way things work. At least they say they'll cover the cost of flying Rob to Dubai and pay for his accommodation, but I'll have to pay for mine myself. Fair enough. Hussein said if we wanted to stay an extra day in Dubai that would not be a problem. Seems generous (if indeed he's telling the truth, but I have my doubts).

All that remains to do now is to get a road permit so we can drive to Dubai and to apply for an alcohol license. Only people above a certain income can buy alcohol, which cannot exceed ten percent per month of their income. Moslems aren't allowed to buy alcohol, though they do in fact frequent the bars. Hussein, with his hand across his heart, assures me he has all this under control and is in fact working very hard on it.

14th August

We reminded Hussein that the promised air-conditioner for the kitchen was long overdue and the kitchen was too hot to cook in. "No problem, Alexa. *Bukrah, Inshallah.*"

God willed the air-conditioner to arrive many tomorrows later and the people installing it left a great gaping hole in the wall where they'd had to break the tiles. I queried when this would be filled: "No problem madam. *Bukrah, Inshallah.*" A few days later your father had to confess to me that he'd seen three cockroaches in the kitchen, after pretending he'd been spraying ants.

I phoned Hussein. "I'll get onto it immediately, Alexa. Don't worry. Just leave it with me." So I left it with him and the next thing was he assured me he'd phoned the maintenance department and the landlord and it would be done by the end of the week. The end of the week came and went ...

Eventually, Jacob, the Indian caretaker of the apartment building turned up with a ladder, a pile of stones and some plaster, to block the hole in the wall. Jacob, sweet man though he is, just nods and says "no problem" to any question. When we saw the way he was stuffing plaster and rocks into the hole and on top of the brand new air conditioner and all over the fridge, we told him to stop and ask the electricians to remove the air conditioner first. Apart from that the part of the hole he could reach was only a small percentage of the entire hole, so it wouldn't have stopped the cockroaches marching through.

At 7.15am one weekend he turned up at the door with the electricians. They took off the air conditioner and Jacob and a companion proceeded to throw rocks and cement into the hole. It did the trick – no more cockroaches, a kitchen cool enough to cook in and once again everyone was happy, if a little frayed around the edges.

The alcohol licence. It's the only thing Hussein has been able to organise properly. He even kept ringing me up to remind me to go to the Police Station to get it and said I could have time off work to do it. Considering how long it had taken him to get the documents ready, I don't know why there was suddenly such urgency. He evidently felt that an alcohol licence was far more important than trivial things like visas, work permits and road passes.

We hung about the Police Station for about an hour while documents were scrutinised, stamped, signed and photocopied, and finally I was issued with the licence which looks like a passport, complete with photo. From there we went to the alcohol shop which is hidden behind a shopping centre and has all the windows painted out. Above the door the only sign is 'Retail Outlet' and a notice that says, 'Only pass holders may enter these premises.' Not the slightest indication of what is sold there. However, inside, it looks like a normal alcohol store, with a very wide range of wines.

We read on my license that we were only permitted to carry the alcohol in the car directly to our place of residence, as long as it was under cover and not on display. It also had to be carried into the apartment under cover. If it was visible in the car we would be stopped by police and fined. We stuffed it in the boot of the car and I wondered whether to cover the bags in ten thick woolly blankets, just to be sure. The licence did state that if in the event of us not being able to transport the alcohol directly home, we had to keep the receipt handy to prove that we had just bought it. Public consumption of alcohol would be asking for an arrest. As we were driving away, I felt the boot of the car glow and vibrate with a neon sign that screamed BOOZE!

As I have no idea when – or even if – we'll eventually get connected to the internet, I'm going into one of the internet cafés later today to send this off before it grows so big it collapses in cyber space. The half dozen phone calls I've made to you weren't nearly long enough, but the mobile phone cards only last ten minutes. Still, it was lovely hearing your voices. It was really sweet of you to go over to see Melanie last week, Olivia, and it was reassuring to know she's coping okay with looking after the house and garden and animals. Even though she was keen I thought it might be a big ask, with two children. I know she'd appreciate you taking the trouble to see her. She must be feeling really scared with the rape trial coming up. I was hugely relieved when you told me she'd said the Police had served a trespass notice on Vincent. Did you know that in the end Melanie wouldn't go with me to the Police Station to sign it, so her mother signed it instead? They told me that Melanie would most likely end up inviting him into the house and in that case the order would become null and void. But I do hope she takes the opportunity to get rid of him once and for all. For a while I was really anxious that her mother would find a way to push him down the stairs one day when he was drunk. Given what she knows about him I can well understand how she feels.

New Zealand already seems a world away, and I sometimes wonder what we're doing here. I feel that I've fallen, like Alice, through to the other side of the looking-glass. I've realised that normality is a construct depending on perspective. However, I still believe we had to leave New Zealand, and the frustrations and strangeness of life here have the effect of giving us something else to think about. I didn't think I could ever smile again, let alone laugh, and yet we've done plenty of laughing here. The beauty of the place makes me catch my breath sometimes too.

I was delighted when you told me you'd bought a digital camera, Sam. Take lots of pictures when you start decorating your house and send them to me. Assuming we EVER get connected to the internet.

Bridging the gap

The tide was out when we arrived at the bay so we rolled up our shorts and waded through warm water to the shore. The two Omani crew members and Mohammed carried all the camping equipment to the beach then the Omanis boarded the boat again, leaving Mohammed and us behind. I was relieved they didn't call out Merry Christmas.

Honey-coloured mountains rose behind the white sand and luminous sea. From the top of a high rock we could see the lights of the city. Jewels in Aladdin's cave. And we talked of the blue and gold minarets, the palaces, the forts, the old, white-latticed houses by the harbour, the market crammed with black-clad women and white-robed men, the clamour of voices, and the seductive drift of frankincense. But from that place to this lay a long curve of empty beach, keening seagulls, an empty sky and an empty ocean. We might have been the only people on earth.

Not quite.

There was Mohammed stacking driftwood as violet light flooded the sky. Within minutes he was wrapped in darkness until he lit the fire and we saw him silhouetted like a shadow-puppet in red and gold flames. As we clambered down the rock, a couple of fishing boats arrived.

The fishermen waved, called to Mohammed, set their nets and took off again, soon swallowed by the night. The wake of their boat agitated the algae and set off sparks of luminescence that edged each wave with silver. Rob grabbed my hand and pulled me laughing into the sea. Our bodies were soon coated with tiny silver stars. We were swimming in stars.

The air was so hot we left the tent open all night and slept in the light of a new moon. I dreamed of paper lanterns and magic castles and sliding down a snow-covered hill. I dreamed of kaleidoscopes and crayons and church bells and fairy tales and dolls' prams and chocolate coins and oranges. I dreamed of a friend killed in a car crash before her 21st birthday. In my dream I tell her she still looks twenty while we have all grown old. I take her hand and feel her soft skin. I say it's terrible that she died so young. She says that's how we look at it from our perspective, but after the moment of dying the perspective is different and you realise that nothing has changed and that your life continues just the same. I argue that I can't see how not having a body is better. She says what you lack in space is made up for by other things.

The dream shook me awake. I wanted to slide back to kaleidoscopes and spinning tops. The sleigh and the snow-man. I tossed and turned. It was the hour when babies slipped into the world and old people slipped out of it, and sometimes those in between. Rob murmured, deep inside dreams of his own. It was stuffy inside the tent, so I slipped outside to breathe in the cooler air. The sky was packed with stars swollen to fat blobs of light. They were so close I reached up to see if I could touch one.

Beth, at seven, stretching up to the top of the Christmas tree with her cut-out star.

I walked into the waves with my baby in my arms. I set her adrift on the sea. A bird flew low overhead.

When I woke again, the world was monochrome. Rob was already in the sea and Mohammed was boiling water on the fire for coffee. The fishermen who'd set the nets the previous night returned to collect them. They waved and sailed away. The sun was not yet up behind the mountains, but amber light had begun to stain the peaks.

Beth at ten, bringing me her cardboard cut-out mountains with a strip of orange tissue paper behind to make the sunrise glow. Beth at twenty, working on Kevin's farm. "It was foggy and I couldn't see the mountains. When the fog cleared and the mountains were visible I knew I was home."

Crabs ran about digging frantically, the males leaving towers of sand to attract females. Tiny pink shells lay scattered, glittering like rubies, along the beach. The sea was a mirror of the sky. I ran in and shattered clouds. The sun rolled over the mountains, painting the sea with light. We swam in liquid gold.

Mohammed waved to let us know he had breakfast ready – fresh croissants, hot coffee and mince pies.

"Merry Christmas!" he shouted, looking pleased with himself. Hoping that's exactly what we wanted to hear.

Rob put his arm around my shoulders. "They're just words," he said.

They weren't Beth's saddles gathering dust in the barn. They weren't her ashes in the earth. They were shadows on a foreign beach, a crackling fire, the smell of coffee, stars in the sea. They were Mohammed's gift to us. We thanked him and said "Merry Christmas" back to him.

I'll get back to you

"Sign here, Alexa. It includes everything we agreed on before you left New Zealand." Hussein, the CEO, slid the contract across his desk.

"Thanks. I'll have it back to you tomorrow."

"Tomorrow? Don't you trust me?"

I glanced at the print-out then drew a diagram to clarify, yet again, the holiday pay, salary, and gratuity to be paid at the conclusion of my twelve-month contract.

He sighed. "Okay, just tell me what to write!"

"Change 'Single air ticket paid back to country of origin on conclusion of contract' to 'Refund for single air ticket ...' considering I've already paid for my own tickets."

"But Alexa, of course we will refund you. We've already agreed to that."

I wasn't convinced, but the more immediate issue was trying to get Omantel to connect the new wiring to the phone.

Next morning one of the Omantel engineers rang to say the lines were connected.

"It's all finished. The line is connected."

"No, it isn't. The cable hasn't been connected."

"Yes, it has. The men fixed it yesterday."

"No. The electricians changed the wiring. They didn't connect it to the phone line."

"Mmmm. I'll get back to you."

A week later Rob rang the manager. "When are the men coming to connect the cable?"

"*Bukrah, Inshallah.*"

Two weeks later Rob asked him where the men were. He said he'd get back to us.

More weeks went by. Finally, I rang and was told he was in a meeting. Then away having his lunch. When I finally nabbed him he was very apologetic; said it was ludicrous we'd been waiting three months for a connection and he would send people out next morning and tell them they had to find the problem and fix it. They came out and decided the problem might be that our modem was too advanced for their system. Next day someone came with an external modem to try it, but it didn't fit, so he said he'd go back and find one that did fit and then get back to us.

Another engineer came out and confessed he was completely stumped and had no idea why the internet wouldn't work. "However, I'm talking to other people and they are working on finding a solution."

I told him a very simple solution would be to just give us another phone line.

"Mrs Alexa has just given me a good idea," he said. "However, there'll be some paperworks first, some departments to get permissions from."

I asked how long that would take. He said when he knew that he'd get back to me.

The engineer had to go away for the weekend, but promised to contact us when he returned. He didn't, so Rob rang him, but he was in a meeting. He promised to ring back. He didn't. Rob rang back the next morning and he said that he was no longer on the case as it had been transferred back to the original pair of engineers. I rang his manager. It was time for losing some cool. When I paused for breath the manager said he would ring the two men concerned and "expedite the matter", and "get back to you." Naturally he didn't and when I tried to ring him again he didn't answer the phone.

Later that day another engineer, who had originally been on the case, rang me and said he was "horrified" to find that three months later our problem had not yet been solved, but he personally would solve it and get back to us. I asked him to say exactly what he intended to do and he said that as everything had been tested and nothing had been found to be at fault the only conclusion he could come to was that it was the exchange. "So we will give you a new phone line and get back to you today, *Inshallah*."

We knew then it really was the end of the line for the phone line. But God had other plans.

"The men are installing the new line as we speak," the engineer shouted down the mobile phone.

When we returned to the flat Rob switched on the computer and to our amazement there was the internet.

Minutes later the engineer rang. "Mrs Alexa. Mr Rob. Thanks be to God, I have solved your problem for you!"

We told him we were immensely grateful, both to God and to him.

Next morning, I reminded Hussein that the extension on Rob's visitor's visa was about to run out.

"Alexa, I am working on this."

"But there's a hefty fine on over-stayers."

He brought his palms to his shoulders. "*We* will pay the fine. If Rob has to leave the country to re-enter on a new visitor's visa *we* will pay his airfare to Dubai. You can go with him. I'll give you time off work. This is the company's problem and *we* will fix it."

The day the visa expired he told Rob he had to fly to Dubai that evening. Philippe, the Director of Studies told him to authorise Rob's air ticket. We walked into the office as this conversation was going on. He handed Rob the phone.

"Pay your air ticket?" squeaked the voice over the receiver. "Where did you get that idea?"

"Hang on! You said …"

"That we would try to help you with your visa problems …"

"Help me with …?"

"… but with this attitude it seems you are very ungrateful …"

When we picked pieces of Rob off the walls and reassembled him, he had only two hours to get his ticket to Dubai.

Philippe sighed. He explained that Hussein had probably been over-ruled by the Sheik who owned the school and didn't want to lose face by admitting it.

While Rob was in Dubai waiting in the airport for a flight back to Oman, I stood by the window of our flat, looking at the cluster of white, flat-roofed houses that snaked up the hill towards the mountains. Washing was drying on lines on some of the rooftops. Sand-covered satellite dishes were visible on others. A couple of street cleaners were sweeping up the plastic bottles and litter that was deposited daily on the streets. There was no grass visible in the neighbourhood, just dusty, sand-coloured earth along the sides of the high-walled, dilapidated houses. From my window I could see inside some of the cracked concrete yards behind the high walls. This year away from everything familiar was meant to help us re-assemble all our broken pieces, but dealing with Hussein felt like falling further down the rabbit hole.

Four months after he'd promised to send the letter he'd written guaranteeing the conditions of my contract to the Sheik it still hadn't been done and he was about to leave the country for a month's vacation. "It isn't actually necessary for the Sheik to sign it, Alexa," he said. "I am a signatory of this company."

"You know as well as I do that unless the Sheik's signature is on a document it's not legal."

"It will be signed and on your desk this afternoon, before I leave."

It wasn't, of course, so I asked the company's accountant, Mahmoud, to come to the school to see me. He said he'd never seen any such letter. Not only that, the Sheik had not signed my contract.

"In that case, whose signature is on the contract?"

He breathed deeply then asked me to send a copy of the contract so he could check out the signature. "But Mrs Alexa, why are you claiming a refund on your airfare back to New Zealand? Hussein told me you wouldn't claim the airfare to New Zealand."

"What?"

"He said you wouldn't claim the return portion because you'd already paid for your flights as part of a round-the-world ticket. You're going to Brazil and the USA when your contract expires, yes?"

"I'm not expecting you to pay for those trips. Just to refund the cost of the fare from Oman back to New Zealand."

"The company doesn't give refunds," he said. "Only tickets. We can give you a ticket at 50% discount of the full fare."

"Hussein gave me a refund of my fare from New Zealand to Oman," I said, "and at the end of my contract I want him to refund the portion of my ticket from Oman to New Zealand, as my contract states."

Mahmoud's frown deepened. "He had no right to give you a refund," he said. "We don't give refunds. Only tickets. I have his letter in my office. It states you agreed not to claim your return airfare. He signed it. I can show you if you like."

"Is *my* signature on that letter?"

"No, but Hussein's is."

"Why would I agree to not claiming my return airfare when it is in my contract, which supposedly has been signed by the Sheik?"

Sweat dripped down his neck. "Mrs Alexa, send me the contract and all your documents by fax and I'll get back to you."

Next morning I sent a twelve-page fax. A week later when he finally answered my call he said he was waiting for Hussein to return so we could all have a meeting with the Sheik. "I'll get back to you with the time of the meeting," he said.

The meeting didn't materialise. Neither did Rob's visa. Hussein said he was trying to arrange an appointment with the Minister to "find a way round this." The appointment didn't materialise either.

Rob was asked to teach a Master of Engineering course at Sultan Qaboos University and a temporary work visa was arranged for him there. We flew to Dubai early on a Wednesday morning and at the airport Rob faxed a copy of the exit stamp back to the Public Relations Officer at the university. The Public Relations Officer told him the visa would be ready on Saturday afternoon "… *Inshallah.*" We were very nervous in case God was extra busy with visas that weekend and Rob might end up staying in Dubai for several days, or weeks, or months, or years, or the rest of his life. However, to our surprise it was ready when it was supposed to be.

Hussein had assured us before he left the country that he had booked a plane ticket and hotel for the teacher we were expecting from Australia. As Philippe was away, I rang Head Office to ask when we could expect him.

"What ticket? What teacher?"

Stifling a scream I said, "We have new classes starting and no teacher. Get him here ASAP."

Rick, the teacher, was whisked from Australia to Oman in a flash. When he arrived at school he told us he had almost not got here because the e-mail from Head Office didn't actually state where it was from and he deleted it. Fortunately, it had also been sent to his father who phoned him to tell him he had to get on a plane the next day. I told him he could have a few hours' sleep before his class started that evening.

Two days later Rick was beaten up at a party by an American marine, after saying something unflattering about President Bush. As the teachers were easing him into a car next morning to take him to hospital a reporter from the local newspaper turned up and demanded an interview about the English programmes the school was offering. I explained the Director of Studies and the CEO were over-seas and suggested she come back in a couple of weeks, after making an appointment.

"I have my article almost completed," she wailed. "I only need to ask you a couple of questions."

An hour later she was still talking and scribbling, but it kept my mind off Rick's smashed face and the consequences if one of those kicks had landed a few centimetres nearer his temple.

The weekend before the Islamic New Year we visited archaeological sites with the Historical Society. People in our group discussed whether or not Saturday or Sunday would be the New Year's Day holiday. The Islamic New Year is based on the cycles of the moon. A committee within one of the Ministries – The Committee of Moon Sightings – had to personally view the new moon before the New Year could be announced. However, my students said they were sure the New Year would be Saturday and so they were all going home to their villages then and would come back to school on Sunday. At midnight on Friday the phone rang. It was Philippe to say Hussein had told him that even though there would be no students on Saturday, the moon had not yet been sighted, so all the teachers had to come to work.

Dawn trek in the Wahiba Desert

Soon after entering the desert we passed a little oasis where the Bedouins lived for a few months each year, harvesting their dates. The rest of the time, Jaber said, they lived in the desert in huts made out of palm leaves, tending their camels and goats. Jaber's car was very rickety and had no seat belts. To get up the high steep-sided dunes he had to let the pressure down on the tyres to avoid getting stuck in the sand. Then he charged up the dunes at breath-stopping speed and down the other side only marginally more slowly. In this way we drove deeper into the desert with its seemingly endless dunes of red-gold sand, scrubby bushes and acacia trees.

We got out of the cars and climbed to the top of a high dune to watch the sun sink and the intensity of light fade from the sky. At the bottom of the dune Jaber and Abdullah built a palm leaf shelter, made a fire and boiled water to make coffee. As the rest of our group finished setting up the tents, Jaber's brother arrived in a truck with our meals, cooked by his mother and sisters – chicken and rice with spices and lemon and coffee with saffron and cardamom. We sat around the campfire eating, talking and laughing as the night darkened and the stars and moon provided the only light.

Just before dawn I stepped outside my tent. The dunes had lost their definition in the grey light and the silence was pervading. In the absence of sound, I became aware of my own breathing. I wondered about the generations of Bedouins who had made their home in that inhospitable terrain over so many centuries, travelling over the dunes on their camels, living out their lives without much change until the 1970s. I had read accounts of Europeans who had explored the desert and said they almost went mad with the silence and loneliness.

Within minutes the dense black night faded to grey. A slice of pink appeared in the east and the red rim of the sun rose above the horizon. It rapidly rolled over the tops of the dunes, its light staining the grey sand with red–gold again and evaporating the early morning chill. We ate our breakfast watching colour return to the desert as the other campers stirred and emerged from their tents too. In the distance a string of camels, led by a Bedouin child, walked along the ridge of dunes towards our camp.

Ten gorgeous creamy yellow camels with huge eyes and lips lay on the sand waiting for us with several Bedouins, including Jaber's father, Said, and his son. They were enormous. When someone started talking about the last time he rode a horse, fell off, and spent the rest of the day in hospital, I almost decided not to go on the trek, but I knew I would have regretted it for the rest of my life.

Finally, we were all mounted and ready to go. The camel I was on had her baby tied to her. I could hear them breathing and see the soft hairs on their lips and the eyelashes around their dark eyes. The Bedouin children learn to ride when they are two years old. They are given camels as pets to look after and bond with. The boy leading the camel I rode was only eight. As we set off I saw the camel nuzzle his head and the child looked up and smiled at her. This almost made me forget I was a very long way from the ground.

We trekked for an hour along the tops of the dunes. Uphill was easy as the camels spread their huge legs to climb. Downhill was trickier because they leaned forward and I ended up wrapped around the camel's hump. The sky was brilliant blue and long shadows lay in the hollows of the dunes. The Wahiba Desert is 12,000 kilometres long. The vastness of wave upon wave of rolling dunes was hard to comprehend. Being in the middle of the ocean must induce the same feeling. Gradually the nervous laughter and chatting stopped and our group was quiet. The silence and space wrapped around us. The only sound came from the camels breathing and a bird singing shrilly in an acacia tree.

Team-building

Monique was small in stature, huge in voice and ego. She managed to offend everyone on the first day of our team-building weekend. When Rick stood up to shake hands she hollered, "Oh you must be the guy who got himself beaten up at the Marine Club?"

And to Rob, "Who the hell are you?"

"Alexa's husband ..."

"Oh, don't say you're somebody's husband. You're a person in your own right!" She turned to yell at the waiter, "Hey, you with the broom-handle lips, bring me some tea."

Next morning over breakfast, as Dom was spluttering about his encounter with her, the door burst open and in she roared like a blistering wind, flaying the skin off everyone within reach. There was a rush for the exit.

At Ras Al Hadd we waited on the beach for the dhow that was going to take us on a cruise along the coastline. No Monique. A collective sigh of relief. But when we embarked, there she was. She whooped and hollered to get everyone's attention and announced that it was she who'd arranged the dhow trip through her boyfriend, Abdul Rahim, who had paid for the trip. "He's a Sheik, you know," she shrieked. "A millionaire. Well, it's his wife who has money, so he has to be discreet."

"Just as well one of them is," I whispered to Kassidy.

Kassidy's mouth dropped open. "Abdul Rahim? A fiendishly attractive Sheik at that!" she said. "But alcoholic. Serial adulterer."

I raised my eyebrows.

"I'll tell you later," she said.

Devlin, Angie, Marty, Kassidy and I stretched out on fat cushions in the stern of the dhow, drifting on turquoise waves, past amber mountains and empty beaches. Latifa, an Iraqi woman from Dev's college, joined us. When she found out I was from New Zealand, she told me she'd tried to emigrate there when Bush invaded Iraq, but her application was rejected so she came to Oman.

"I grew up in a society that educated women," she said. "We had careers. We travelled. We could choose to marry or not. But now …" She turned her palms upwards.

We fell silent and watched Rob, Dom and Rick pulling on their snorkelling gear. Someone turned up the radio. The haunting rhythms of Arabian music drifted on the air.

"I hope it's all to your liking," Monique bellowed, steaming up to the helmsman. She rubbed her bare shoulder against his, batted her eyelids at him and whispered throatily in Arabic. He looked mortified, but moved away and let her take over the wheel.

"Isn't this fantastic folks?" she screeched. "We owe it all to my boyfriend. He's a Sheik, you know!"

As the dhow skimmed over the waves someone asked if she knew where the rocks were. "Hey folks," she thundered. "Drop the doom. Enjoy the boom."

I tapped her on the shoulder.

She glared at me. "What's your problem?"

"I don't have a problem. I just want you to move away from the wheel."

The helmsman looked as though he'd been whacked on the head. I pointed to the wheel. He didn't understand my words, but he was in no doubt about my meaning. He nodded and took over the wheel, staring grimly ahead.

"You can't do that!" Monique yelled. "My boyfriend paid for this. He's a Sheik."

I gripped her shoulders and moved her to one side.

She hovered, throbbing, smoke curling from her ears and nostrils, sparks ricocheting off the top of her head. Devlin carried on his conversation about Celtic civilisations. He knew how to spin a good yarn. Monique turned to Kassidy and asked about her sea-sickness, but when Kassidy began to tell her she immediately interrupted, "Oh don't talk about your insecurities, you'll spoil it for everyone else!" She threw one more acid-filled glare in my direction before stomping off to the far end of the deck.

The boat anchored and we all jumped out to go snorkelling. I thought I saw Monique drop into the water behind me, but when I counted heads hers wasn't there. Back on the dhow I saw her curled up in a corner by herself.

Kassidy's roof

Kassidy and Devlin, just back from the TESOL ARABIA conference in Dubai, roared through the door of the Teachers' Room like a couple of nor'west winds. Their fury was hot enough to blister the paintwork.

"This … *cheapskate* bloody *company* …" Kassidy spat.

"… put us in the *cheapest* friggin' hotel they could find …" Devlin continued while Kassidy struggled for breath.

"… and even the taxi driver says to us, 'You sure madam?' And when we get there …" Kassidy pushed her long red hair back from her sweating face with both hands.

"… it's a pay-by-the-hour brothel!" Devlin finished.

Rick, Angie, Dom, Marty and I exploded with laughter.

"Look! Look!" shrieked Kassidy, rolling up her sleeves. Her arms were covered in small red lumps. "*Prostitutes! Hairy sailors! Hordes* of smelly labourers! I even wore my specs and flapped conference papers just in case they thought … but *fleas!*" Her pained face started us all off laughing again.

"At first I thought, okay we can manage for two nights," said Devlin, "but when I get out the shower there's a message for me from the desk to say Her Ladyship here has checked out. She rings me and says she's booked into the Millennium …"

"… where the rest of the delegates were I might add," Kass cut in, "*Flown* there too. Not made to *drive* eight hours from Muscat to Dubai like us poor sods!"

"So I pack my bag and go over to the Millennium where I'm about to say a word or two to Madam about being a friggin' Drama Queen …"

"… and then he sees *these* …" Kassidy held out her arms again.

"And now," finished Devlin with theatrical calm, "I'm on my way to Hussein's office where I'll throw these friggin' receipts at him and if I'm not reimbursed immediately, I'm outta here on the next friggin' plane!" He squared his shoulders, tilted his chin and strode out of the room and down the stairs.

The rest of us collapsed over our desks.

"But …" Kassidy looked over her shoulder to make sure Devlin wasn't within hearing range, "I have to say … it was the *fleas* that bonded us! You know, on the drive up, he admitted he hadn't been all that keen on the idea of travelling to Dubai with me! This Drama Queen business. *Me!*" she said, incredulous. "I blame Philippe of course, feeding Dev all those lies about me – a Director of Studies should be more professional than that, even if he does feel threatened by me because I'm better qualified than him, but anyway, sod Philippe. When Dev saw the *lumps* …"

The door opened.

"My place, tonight. The roof. 7.30," Kassidy whispered.

Philippe stuck his head in the room. "What's all the racket about?"

Kassidy had set dozens of white candles on the ledges around the flat roof of her apartment building. There was a large plastic table in the centre buckling under the weight of plates of prawns, smoked salmon, cheeses, grapes, Arabian bread and bottles of wine. Kassidy was busy lighting the candles when we arrived.

"Wow!" Rob and I exclaimed at the same time.

"Hafiz's idea," Kassidy said. "Magical, isn't it?"

I found a spot for the chocolate cake I'd brought and Rob made space for his wine.

"There's enough booze here already to last a week!" he said.

"Yeah. That's the thing about the Alcohol License," said Kassidy. "I always buy more than my limit, just on principle. The little treasure in the shop I go to even discounts for me so I can have over my quota." To me she whispered, "Hafiz puts lighted candles on the steps up to the apartment just before I come home from work. And *rose* petals in my bath!"

"What a treasure!" I said. "Give me some of those incense thingies and I'll light them for you."

"He is. And I'm grateful," she agreed, handing me the incense, the matches and a glass of wine and grabbing one of her cats off the table just as it was about to swipe a prawn. She opened the door to the stairs, shoved the cat out and closed the door. "No manners that one. Found him in a bin. Near death! Anyway ... Hafiz *is* sweet, it's just that, you know, he's twenty-five. My last lover, Abdul Rahim, was thirty-eight and I thought *that* was pushing it a bit!" She grinned. "He's a Sheik, you know!"

I choked on my wine. "Monique!"

Kassidy handed me a tissue to mop up the wine I'd spluttered onto the front of my dress.

"Incredibly handsome man," she said, "But he collects women like racing trophies. Well, don't they all? Rich men I mean. So until Hafiz, the Sheik was my last lover ... oh, apart from that German I got off the internet, but I don't count him. Said he was forty-nine. Not that I can complain. Told him I was thirty-nine."

I raised an eyebrow.

"So ..." Kassidy interrupted herself to eat a piece of bread and handed me another handful of tissues. "This bread is heavenly! It's that new bakery in Al Medina. The manager was a student of mine last year. Used to be in the Secret Police. Yes, truly! He told me his dream was to make the best bread in Muscat. Anyway, Hafiz. Well, Hafiz seemed so ... so *uncomplicated* ... but ... oh oh he calls me 'his *girl*'! I don't know, maybe it wasn't such a good idea to let him move in with me. He's started to read my e-mails over my shoulder."

I pictured Hafiz, spectacular in his new black *dishdasha* and black turban at Kass's fiftieth birthday party, dark eyes besotted with Kass in her green silk dress, her red hair tumbling like a mane around her shoulders.

Footsteps clattered up the stone steps and Angie, Devlin and Rick arrived with more food, wine and beer. Marty and Dom followed with their CD player and a bag full of CDs. Rob handed everyone a drink and they dived into the food. The strains of Tagore's *Gift of Love* wove soft threads around the excited chatter.

Clouds floated like pink balloons in the lemon sky. Green parrots argued over our heads on their way home to roost. The heat of the day was released from the concrete floor and mingled with the scent of jasmine from the garden below and frangipani from the smoky swirls of incense. From up here, we could see right over the golden domes and green and blue minarets, white and cream and pink apartment blocks and new shopping malls, all the way down to the sea, which lay as flat and polished as a sheet of turquoise glass. The streetlights were strung like bright beads along the beachfront.

"… and I called him a *liar* and a *cheat!*" Devlin was thumping the table, reliving the scene in Hussein's office, "and he's saying to me, 'Come on Dev, we can sort this out', and I'm saying to him, 'Don't you Dev me, you get on that phone *now* to Abdal-Hakim and you tell him I want my money reimbursed, or I'm on the next plane back to Dublin! And he's telling me it isn't his fault - it's Mahmoud's - and then he rings Abdal-Hakim and he says, 'Abdal-Hakim, we have a problem.' And I hear Abdal-Hakim say over the phone, 'Give him the money, we can't afford to lose another one. Not before the exams!' So he had no choice!"

"YAY!" Marty applauded.

Kassidy refilled our glasses and we toasted Dev's success.

Angie perched on a ledge and told the story of when Hussein was sent to London to recruit English teachers for the college in the desert where she works. "And he picks up this girl in a bar. I think she was a dancer or something. Russian. Anechka. And he brings her over here and sticks her in front of a class. Well, she's in floods of tears every day because the little darlings know perfectly well she hasn't got a clue, so the rest of us spend our breaks and evenings helping her with lesson plans."

"And the next thing," Devlin broke in, "is that his wife, who's back home in Egypt, gets wind of something and causes a stink and suddenly Hussein is transferred to Muscat. Three months later, so is Anechka. The teachers all complained to Philippe and got nowhere of course, so they went down to see Mahmoud at Head Office and told him that she only ever turned up three minutes before her lessons and took off the second they were over while the rest of them were not allowed to leave the school till 4.30."

"And Mahmoud's comment," interrupted Angie, "was … 'I would not want *my* daughters taught by a girl who lives in an adulterous liaison'."

"Hypocritical bastard!"

"So the upshot," continued Angie, "was that her visa was not renewed at the end of her contract. The Sheik refused to give her a letter of release, so that meant she couldn't get another job in Oman, and so, bye bye Anechka. And Hussein drowned his sorrows, as they say, down at the pub."

"I signed my contract two weeks ago," frowned Rick. "Is it worth the paper it's written on?"

Rob and I looked at each other.

"Debbie!" Angie and Dev chorused.

The day we'd bought the car, Debbie asked us to take her to the bank. She had completed her contract and was due to fly to South Africa the following day. When she read her bank statement she burst into tears.

"*He promised!*"

Back at school she flew into his office, emerging ten minutes later red-faced and frothing at the mouth. Philippe led her into his office to get her out of earshot of the students. That evening, at her goodbye dinner, she told us Philippe said he'd write to the Sheik explaining that it wasn't feasible for her to come back from South Africa at the end of her vacation just to collect her gratuity, even though, strictly speaking, the company was acting according to Labour Law, so maybe they could make an exception and just let her have it before she left.

"Fat chance!" said Dev, "And why should Philippe queer his own pitch? He's on a nice little package. By the way, him and Mike?"

"Oh oh oh … don't go there!" interrupted Kass. "More wine anyone?"

"Look, Philippe's job is to keep bums on seats. If the teachers are qualified, that's a bonus," said Devlin.

"Oh God, Al Sayida!" said Kassidy. "Think broad Glaswegian accent, black abaya, pierced eyebrows, tattoos on her hands and neck."

"You're joking!"

"No. Serious. She came for an interview last year. I'd actually had coffee with her the previous week and she told me she had this interview coming up and wanted some tips, the right jargon, to impress the Director of Studies. Imagine how disconcerted I was to see that her interview was at our school! Half an hour later Philippe comes in, beaming from ear to ear and tells me how well-qualified she is, a Masters in Applied Linguistics, with Distinction, no less. I said, oh *Philippe*, darling, she's lived in Oman for twenty years, been married three times, twice to Omanis. She changed her name to Thuraya, insists on being called Al Sayida – your Royal Highness. Philippe, I said, *Philippe*, her degree is *fake*! And of course, you know how Philippe is 'Oh no no no Kassidy, you've got it all wrong' so I showed him the website of the so-called university where she got her so-called degree. It's one of those places where you can buy a degree and even state which grade you want to graduate with. Presumably you pay a bit more if you want a distinction. It even showed the campus and all the courses it was supposed to have, none of which, including the campus, exist."

Marty stopped arranging hibiscus blossoms in her hair for a moment and asked, incredulous, "But *my* qualifications had to be signed and stamped by a million government departments in Australia before I sent them to Oman."

"Look," said Devlin, "we've had backpacking tourists that Hussein has met in the pub and convinced to do a spot of teaching, and then he hid them in the loo when the Ministry did one of their random checks."

We looked at Dom who stopped munching mid-prawn.

"What's your Masters in again?" teased Marty. "Electronics will of course really help him teach the past perfect and future conditional!"

"It's all right darling, we're not getting at you *personally,*" Kassidy said. "And of *course* you're not going to turn down the offer, but puleeeaaase …!"

"Because," continued Devlin looking at Marty, "to answer your question, the good ones do a runner."

"And this doesn't encourage the company to examine their work practices?" Rob asked.

Devlin and Kassidy fell about laughing.

"Oh my *precious!*" squealed Kassidy, "welcome to the world of TEFL teaching. Of course, with your lecturing job at the university and your PhD you are not going to be subjected to the same treatment as we lowly BAs. In my last job at the Teachers' College I had an argument with the Head of School and he actually said, 'Who the hell do you think you are? You only have a BA. I have a PhD!' It was him and his bloody PhDness that made me decide to do a Masters."

When we finished laughing, Kassidy continued, "Hussein's proposed solution to the absconding teachers was to confiscate our passports which were to be given back to us at the airport, *after* we'd returned the Labour Card and Alcohol License!"

"But for once," Devlin interrupted, "even Philippe stood up to him."

"So how come *you* stay?" Rob asked.

But we already knew the answer.

Angie came on a two-year contract to make enough money to put her son, Matt, through university. Three weeks after she started teaching, Matt, who'd stayed behind in Edinburgh, was killed after being hit by a car on his way home from the library late one night. Angie renewed her contract for a further two years because she didn't know what else to do. "I think, sometimes, that at the end of my contract, he'll still be waiting for me," she said.

Devlin came to rebuild his bank balance after his divorce. "Two more years and I'll be out of here," he kept saying. "If I can hack it just another couple of years I can retire on what I've saved."

Rick's business, selling surfing gear on the Gold Coast went bust. He was sparing on the details, but hinted at a spell in detox. He did a basic course in TEFL to get qualifications to teach English as a Foreign Language and went to Saudi Arabia. After getting caught up in a crowd on its way to a public beheading he did a runner. Thankfully, he was sparing on those details too.

I looked at him remembering his arrival in Oman a week late because Hussein hadn't organised his visa in time. I remembered the call from Marty. She was crying, so it was hard to decipher what she was saying. *Rick! Bar! Americans! Beaten up! An Omani! Hafiz!*

By the time Rob and I streaked over to Rick's flat Marty and Dom were shoehorning him into their car to take him to hospital. His face was a purple balloon, his right eye split and needing stitches and he could hardly walk. He said the Americans had kicked him in the head.

Dom found the name of someone in the British Embassy who would intercede in the 'incident' with Rick and the Americans. He and Marty took Rick home with them.

"Reporting this sort of thing is fraught with problems," Kassidy had said, dialling the Embassy, cigarette dangling from the corner of her mouth. She talked to the British Diplomat who had spoken to people from the American Embassy. Three courses of action looked likely: a diplomatic investigation through the nearest Australian Embassy in Riyadh; an investigation by the Police and Omani law would be applied; an apology and settlement from the American Embassy.

Over the next few days there were meetings with various officials and then suddenly the 'incident' evaporated and Rick went silent on the topic. He received a letter from Abdal-Hakim advising him that as alcohol had been involved the company would not pay his medical bills.

"Arseholes!" he exploded.

"Think yourself lucky they didn't put you on the next plane back home!" Kassidy said.

"Or worse!"

Hafiz, who'd been involved in all the embassy meetings as a witness to the fight, became as tight-lipped as Rick. He did, however, start turning up at all the rooftop parties. And a week ago he moved in with Kassidy.

Devlin started filling us in on the details of Monique's sudden and mysterious illness which necessitated a stay in hospital before she was swiftly dispatched back to Canada a week ago.

"... and I quote – '*we don't want her dying on us here*' – and as soon as she was discharged from hospital they put her on the cheapest flight available which involved a ten-hour wait for connections in some God-forsaken airport."

Dom stood up and poured himself another wine. "Hey guys, can we change the record? I came to Oman to enjoy myself. Marty and I have bought furniture. Plants. I didn't come just for the money either. I value the opportunity to contribute to the development of education here."

Everyone stopped speaking and stared at him.

Marty looked at us with an expression between a smile and a wince.

Devlin raised his glass. "To *altruism*," he said.

Kassidy jumped up and poured more wine for everyone to fill the awkward silence, whispering to me, "Mysterious illness? He's a *Sheik* you know."

My third choking fit was masked by the appearance of Hafiz carrying two of Kassidy's cats under his arms and followed by a short man in a green and gold kaftan and black eyeliner. He introduced the man as Crispian, a teacher from the British Council in Dubai, in Muscat for a holiday. Hafiz explained he'd met him in the supermarket earlier that day and invited him to the party.

"I was a lost soul," added Crispian.

"Then you've come to the right place," said Devlin, raising his glass again. "To all us lost souls. Or is that loose marbles? Whatever. Welcome!"

Hafiz handed the cats to Kassidy and kissed her. As Devlin began the story of the brothel, the fleas, the meeting with Hussein, all over again for Hafiz's benefit, Kassidy dispatched the cats through the door and poured more wine in my glass.

"Do *you* ever invite strangers you've just met in the supermarket to a party?" she asked.

"Er …"

"No. Nor do I. That's what I mean when I say there's a lot about Hafiz I don't understand."

Hafiz was from Zanzibar. Swahili was his first language, Arabic his second and English his third. Charming and handsome, he worked as a receptionist at a five-star hotel. Whenever he came to a party he brought with him an assortment of friends and cousins. But tonight's guest?

Kassidy's Italian neighbour, Aldabella, arrived with a basket full of bread and more red wine. Hearing part of Devlin's story she begged him to start at the beginning. I felt a twinge of guilt about Dom, who pulled Marty away from the group to dance. Rick was standing by himself, throwing back beer after beer. Rob wandered over to talk to him. Crispian hovered in the shadows, watching Aldabella, who was punctuating Dev's story with "*No! You're not serious!* I can't *believe!*"

Bella came to Muscat twenty years ago then stayed on after her divorce. A local businessman 'sponsored' her so she could keep her work visa.

"She drives into the desert with her sponsor once a month," Kassidy said. "I said to her, '*Aldabella*' I said, 'how *could* you? Even for ten minutes once a month?' And you know what she said? 'Not ten minutes, *two!*'."

"Poor Bella," I said and turned away to look at the sea.

At first I thought the sparks flashing on the waves were reflections of the slice of moon pinned to the night sky, or lights from the palm trees in front of the restaurants along the beach. Then wave after wave of fluorescent green and blue and orange light flashed in the water as the algae was disturbed by the motion of the sea. It was so beautiful my breath caught in my throat.

Behind me Kassidy was launching into her hammam saga. Last week we were having dinner with her and she spent the evening deciding whether to keep her dental appointment or go to the beauty salon to have her nail extensions repaired. I recommended that she go to the dentist and afterwards, treat herself to the Moroccan Hammam. "You'll love it!" I enthused, "Angie told me about it. It's pure indulgence."

Next morning I walked into the Teachers' Room and asked how she'd liked it.

She was leaning over her desk, her long hair swept up in a ponytail, her green eyes sparkling. "Er … you tell me first," she said.

"It was great. Very relaxing."

"*How* relaxing … *exactly?*"

She now had everyone in paroxysms with her re-enactment of our conversation and her description of what went on in the steam room.

"Well, I said to myself, *Alexa* recommended this."

"Hey!" I protested, "What did *you* do to let her think it was okay?"

"Nothing! Truly! But this is a natural consequence of a segregated society, don't you think?"

Hafiz stood up and wandered over to the edge of the roof and looked out to sea. Crispian stood beside him. Soon they were deep in conversation.

"But *honestly!* If you close your eyes, there's no *differ-ence!* She could just as easily have been a man! In fact, to be quite honest, it was *better!*"

More howls of laughter. Dom danced with intense concentration.

"So … this hammam … are you going again?" Rick asked with studied casualness.

Kassidy's face arranged itself in a saintly expression.

"You know, you're just like Patsy in *Absolutely Fabulous*," Rick said.

She grinned, "I'm just a chameleon sweetie. Well, with *my* life …"

She told us she'd lived in Tuscany for twenty years, married to an Italian millionaire. After she'd had an ectopic pregnancy her husband had a vasectomy to make sure there were no more mistakes.

"He then became a serial adulterer and I divorced him," she said. "Italian law did not allow me to claim any of our property or joint finances so I went back to London and drove taxis for four years to put myself through university."

"So how come you haven't found anybody else?" asked Rick.

Kassidy laughed. "*Darling*, I didn't meet anyone I even wanted to spend a weekend with, let alone my whole life. Then one day I turned around to find I was forty-nine and alone. That's when I tried the internet dating thing. In the Middle East you don't meet anyone in the normal way."

As Kass told her story her hands were in constant motion, punctuating and emphasising, folding and unfolding, flicking back her hair, stroking her arms. Her gestures, hair and eyes were feline. At school she played with Hussein as if he were a mouse. Philippe, immune to female charms, was intimidated by her intelligence.

In my first week at the school there was a staff meeting with Hussein and Philippe. Philippe had asked Kassidy to prepare a workshop on teaching phonemics, as pronunciation was the project she was working on for her Masters dissertation. Kassidy wrote on the whiteboard in phonemic script: *The most important things in life are manicures, pedicures and massages.* Hussein arranged his face in what he presumably thought was a suitably academic expression and pretended he could read the phonemes. Philippe read the sentence aloud then glared at Kassidy. She blew him a kiss. I felt a bubble of laughter form in the pit of my stomach and expand until I felt I would burst with the effort of keeping it inside. Fortunately, neither Hussein nor Philippe noticed. But Kassidy did. After the meeting she invited me to go roller-blading with her in the carpark of the Intercontinental that evening.

"*Roller-blading?*"

"It's the only way to keep slim at this time of year, darling."

In the dark, empty carpark, holding our blades, we collapsed like a couple of hysterical schoolgirls.

At 3.00am, Rob offered to help Kassidy carry the dishes and remains of the food down to her kitchen, but Aldabella said she'd do it in the morning as she was an early bird. Crispian, who hadn't said a word to anyone except Hafiz, left with no goodbyes. Rick was too drunk to drive so Angie gave him a lift home. Dom packed up his CD player in silence. Marty looked at him and rolled her eyes. She whispered to Kassidy, "Let me know the next time you're thinking of going back to that hammam."

Devlin tried to persuade us to attend another team-building weekend at the end of the month. "It's called strikin' while the iron is hot, me darlins. I made Hussein agree to pay for it to make up for the brothel business. Jebel Akdar! You haven't lived until you've sat on top of the green mountain and watched the sun break through the early morning mist. It's like watchin' God creatin' the world."

Kassidy walked with us to the parking lot and blew kisses and waved goodbye as each car left. Rob and I were the last to go. I wound down the passenger window and saw Hafiz lighting candles on the steps. Until Hafiz moved in Kassidy had a system set up that turned on her CD player as she opened her front door, and switched on her lamps as she walked into the flat, and activated the voice of her computer so she heard: "Good evening, Kassidy, I hope you've had a nice day."

Kassidy noticed me watching Hafiz. Her eyes gleamed. She flicked back her hair.

"Alexa, believe me, I'm not flattered. This is the Gulf. I could install a revolving door in my bedroom."

I smiled. "See you tomorrow."

As we moved off, I saw her framed in the wing mirror. She gave a final wave then turned and ran lightly up her illuminated steps.

The stone

Three hundred kilometres south-east of Muscat, Egyptian vultures glided above the Eastern Hajar Mountains, and burnt-toffee peaks sliced into the milky sky. Gravel plains and arid valleys lay on the inland side, a vast sandy plain on the east, and to the south the rolling red sand dunes of the Wahiba Desert. Herons and cormorants waited at the edge of the Arabian Sea, which glittered with hard blue light.

The dirt road dropped vertically into the ravine and rose almost as steeply up the other side, where clumps of dun-coloured houses squatted on the cliffs. A battered utility truck, stuffed with turbaned, white-robed villagers, hurtled out of a cloud of red dust straight towards us. It missed our rented Land Cruiser by a centimetre. The men – one of whom was hanging onto a goat – shouted greetings, laughing at our ashen faces. I clutched the stone in my hand. Rob blew out his breath, "Bloody Hell!"

Still shaking, we crawled through the narrow, winding streets of the village of Bimmah, steering warily around donkeys and goats that wandered at will. Just as oblivious were the women in bright red, green and orange dresses and veils who sauntered across the track with baskets on their heads. Blood was spattered over several doorsteps from the *Eid Al Adha* sacrifices and ran into congealed puddles in the gutters. Outside one house a family was helping to carve up a goat strung from a tree. For some reason it made me think of Amina.

Amina came from the Al Mahri tribe which was reputed to have lived in the city of Ubar before it suddenly disappeared, centuries ago, into the desert sands. In the 1990s explorers, with the help of NASA satellites and Bedouin folklore, located the ruins. It was an underground river, the archaeologists said, which had steadily eroded the limestone on which the city had been built, causing it to collapse. Amina disagreed. It was the wrath of God, she said, punishing the inhabitants for their undisciplined lifestyle.

When she returned to the Language Centre last week, after completing only two weeks of her maternity leave, none of the men gave any sign of noticing her grey face streaked with tears, nor did they lift their heads from their books when she kept leaving the class to disappear into the prayer room. Fayza, Amal, Thuraya and Fatma stayed behind when the men left for their coffee break.

"She is from Salalah, Mrs Alexa," said Amal, "But even for a woman from that region this is not normal behaviour. Two weeks! We are worried about her. In our hostel we hear her crying all night, but when we try to talk to her about it she denies it and says she is okay."

I promised I would talk to her myself and asked Amina to come to my office.

In answer to my questions she said, "My father says I must finish my Academic English course."

"But you're twenty-five," I said. "Isn't that decision yours?"

She wiped her face with the sleeve of her *abaya.* She, alone of all the female students, had no embroidery on her sleeves to relieve the plainness of her black robe. And where her classmates' robes were fitted at the waist, Amina's – from Saudi Arabia, she informed me – concealed her tall, graceful figure completely. Which was why none of us at the school had realised she was pregnant, let alone that she had given birth.

"If I don't pass my exams," she wept, "I won't be able to go to Australia to do my postgraduate study. My whole family's depending on me. It's just that I didn't know I would feel like this. I thought I could just hand him over to my mother." Her tears splashed onto my desk. "But I can't stop thinking about him."

"Could you fly back home at the weekends?" I asked.

Amina tucked a stray hair under her *Hijab.* Her fingers were long and slender. Like Beth's.

"Not until after the exams." She took a tissue from the box I gave her and mopped her eyes. "But I can still feel his skin next to mine. My whole body aches to see him, smell him, touch him." She glanced up at me, "Can you understand what I mean, Mrs Alexa? Am I imagining this?"

"Yes, I do understand what you mean," I said. "And no, you're not imagining it."

Her face relaxed. "So you have children too?"

I nodded.

"How many?"

I hesitated. Since my arrival in Oman I'd wondered what I would say if someone asked me this question. Now that someone had, I didn't know how to answer. Amina was watching me, waiting.

"Three," I said.

Her smile broadened. "Are any of them my age?"

"Beth – my youngest," I said, "would have been the same age as you now."

Amina looked into my face.

"I'd like to see her photo," she said at last. "Will you bring me one?"

I promised I would.

The woman carving up the goat saw me watching and waved. I stared at her pink satin dress.

"The blood! How on earth will she wash it off?"

Rob reached over and squeezed my hand.

Between the villages of Bimmah and Shab we spotted a tiny cove of white sand between low cliffs. Behind the beach lay the ruins of an ancient mud-brick town that had been part of a thriving port when Marco Polo visited.

"Perfect timing," said Rob. "It'll get dark soon."

There was plenty of driftwood around to make a fire and while I boiled up the kettle and heated our food Rob set up the tent. We sat cross-legged on the rapidly cooling sand and ate our meal in silence as the sky turned navy and a huge orange moon rolled above the sea. The surf broke with tiny sparks of luminescent light. There was no sound but our breathing. Since Rob had found the stone this morning he'd hardly said a word. I moved closer to him and turned the stone in my hand, pushing its sharp edges into my skin.

This morning we'd watched the sun rise over the sea, because on this day of all days we needed to see colour spill over the earth. We walked past deep holes dug by nesting turtles and over the tractor tyre tracks that their flippers had gouged in the sand. We found piles of broken egg shells at the bottom of the holes.

"Let's hope one of them made it to the sea," Rob said. "Then after twenty-five years it'll find its way back to where it was born." He picked up a stick and drew a heart in the sand around a cluster of empty shells.

"What a waste," I said, counting around two hundred eggs.

"Just part of a cycle," Rob said, writing our initials inside the heart.

We peeled off our clothes and waded gingerly over the stones until we were up to our necks in the sea. Seabirds circled and dived. The sun blazed. Floating on my back in the warm salty water I thought of a friend who had once described the hours he'd spent in the sea after his boat capsized in a storm. As he waited to be rescued the world became the boat he was clinging to and only that moment had any substance. He felt, he said, outside of time. I never fully understood what he meant, until now.

Outside of time. On this day. At this time. Two years ago. In New Zealand.

Beth asks for music. She discusses a racehorse with Vincent and tells him she wants to train a white horse when she gets better. She asks me several times who came through the door and I say there's no one else here, just the seven of us. She touches everyone and checks their names, then asks Melanie, "What sound does a bear make when it's stung by a bee?" We think it's a riddle, but Beth says she doesn't know the answer either. I ask her why she thought of it and she says she has no idea.

The two nurses decide to leave as she seems so much better now. She can breathe and she's laughing and joking. Her face is a better colour. I say goodbye to them on the porch. When I go back into the living room Melanie is telling Beth that she and Vincent will stay overnight so Rob and I can get some sleep. Beth smiles and thanks her, then nestles the side of her face into the chair and closes her eyes. As I sit down opposite her I see her chest is still. We put our faces close to her mouth and nose and feel the tiniest whisper of air. Rob finds a pulse in her neck beating very faintly. My heart is beating so hard I think it will burst. Vincent and Melanie slip outside and wait on the verandah. The nor-wester roars through the trees whipping up the autumn leaves. Rob and I hold Beth's hands.

Beneath the hills wild horses graze in the moonlight. The lead mare lifts her head and pricks her ears. The colts and fillies stop chasing each other's shadows. Foals stand closer to their mothers. The old ones stop grazing. They all watch the lead mare, and wait. The earth holds its breath. Beth's pulse flutters like a moth's wing, and is gone. I go outside to tell Vincent and Melanie and they say they know because the wind has died.

I don't sleep that night and next morning I move around as if trapped in glass. In the middle of a conversation with Olivia and Sam a sound slides from my throat. It rises to a wail. Wave upon wave of wailing, from a place deep inside in my body. I have never heard such a sound in my life and I can't believe it's coming from me. Rob, Olivia and Sam can do nothing but hold me. A fantail taps on the window. As Beth's friends start arriving the fantail circles around their heads.

I floated in the water like a foetus, my arms curled around my knees. Rob knelt on the sand with the sea up to his chin. He gave a long, shuddering sigh like the exhalation that comes after learning the expected bad news is good news. Or the relief when a truck misses your car by a fraction.

The surf hissed. A seagull flew over our heads, its long mournful keening breaking the silence of the deserted beach.

"Do you remember," I said, "when I was in labour? You suggested playing scrabble to keep my mind off the contractions. I thought you were joking! Then you put your hand in the bag of letters and brought out a B."

Rob nodded.

"I knew then our baby would be a girl."

Rob laughed. "If we'd had a boy you'd have convinced yourself the B was for boy."

"No. I knew it was B for Beth."

"Coincidence," Rob said, "just coincidence." Then, "Ouch! These shells are bloody sharp!"

He reached down into the water and brought up a flat, oval stone that fitted into the palm of his hand. "It cut me! It's covered in limpets." He turned it over. His brow creased. He stared at it in silence.

"What's wrong?" I asked.

He held out the stone.

In the middle, where the limpets had dropped off, there was a raised pattern of white calcification. Shaped into a perfectly formed B.

Sitting under the stars on the beach in front of our campfire I held the stone between my hands and stared into the flames.

"In ancient Persia when someone first saw oil trickle out of the desert they didn't understand what it was," I said. "They thought it was some kind of water and when it ignited, they believed the fire was sacred. They didn't believe the flame just went out. They thought it died, like the soul leaving the body."

Rob touched my arm and pointed to the sea. The little sparks from the agitation of the algae had become flashes of light that ran along the length of each wave. The sea was ablaze with white fire. As we stared, struck dumb by the beauty, a large dark shape emerged from the water. A giant turtle. She dragged herself across the sand, stopping to check out sites to dig a hole, then headed directly to our tent and started digging beside it. With a sigh, she began the long process of shovelling out sand with her front flippers. Hardly daring to breathe we edged closer, and by the light of the moon we watched the turtle lay her eggs.

After two hours the exhausted creature covered her nest with sand. Her task completed, she turned around and lumbered back to the sea. We followed hand in hand, and watched her swim away. Pieces of moon floated on the water where she disappeared beneath the waves.

The desert wind and the tinkling of the camel's bell

Tendrils of white smoke spiralled upwards from hundreds of clay frankincense burners on the stalls that lined the *souk.* The smoke mingled with the scent of jasmine and sandalwood and filled the warm evening air with fragrance.

The Frankincense *Souk* in Salalah, in southern Oman, was reputed to be the best place to buy frankincense in the whole of Arabia. Rows of women in black *abayas* and *burqas* looked at me hopefully, calling out *"Merhaba"* (welcome) as I walked by their stalls, feeling self-conscious in my blue jeans and pink t-shirt. I wished I had thought to cover my arms, which seemed to extend in acres of bare flesh as I reached out to take some yellow crystals a young woman held out to me in a woven palm-leaf basket.

Only the woman's hands and her kohl-outlined eyes were visible. She gestured at me to smell the crystals, then sprinkled a couple of them over a piece of hot charcoal in a little clay burner. I breathed in the heady scent and she beckoned Rob to do the same. Already overwhelmed, he was trying hard not to breathe at all. He held out some money to pay for what I had chosen, hoping that might encourage me to leave before he passed out. The woman covered her hand with her *abaya* before she took the money from him. I turned to see a man in a blue turban and long white *dishdasha* approaching.

"Good evening," he boomed, "I'm Abdullah."

Grinning at our startled expressions he explained he was the guide we'd asked our hotel receptionist to find to take us on the frankincense trail next day. He stretched out his arm to shake Rob's hand. I didn't offer my own in case he was embarrassed. However, when he extended his hand to me, I shook it, with the prickling sensation of dozens of pairs of curious female eyes watching us.

Next morning Abdullah collected us in his battered old Land Cruiser and drove us out of Salalah into the Dhofar Mountains. Salalah, 1,000 kilometres south of Muscat, was the second biggest city in Oman, bordered by Al Wusta in the east, the Arabian Sea to the south, the Yemen in the south west, and Saudi Arabia across the desert known as the Empty Quarter. As we hurtled round a corner on the motorway Abdullah slammed on his brakes to avoid colliding with a camel. He heard our gasps and reassured, "Don't worry, I'm used to this! It's not possible to fence off the desert, you see."

Abdullah explained that 5,000 years ago the south of Oman was the centre of the world's frankincense trade. The climate, hot and dry for most of the year, but lush with rain and mists during the monsoon season from June to September, provided the ideal growing conditions for the little twisted trees known as *olibanuin*, which grew on the desert side of the Dhofar mountains.

We pulled into the side of the road and headed toward a grove of the trees. Abdullah made an incision in one to show us how the sap ran out and hardened into a crystal. "They are collected after two weeks and sold in the markets. Omanis buy them to scent their homes and clothes. In ancient times frankincense was in great demand in the temples of Rome and Mesopotamia. A whole year's supply of frankincense was burned at the funeral of Nero's wife." He turned to Rob. "Some historians say that at least one of the Magi started the journey to Bethlehem from Southern Oman."

Dusty and hot, we stopped in Razat, where springs flowed from the mountains. Abdullah spotted some of his friends there who'd been selling goats in the market that morning. They were cooking rice and fish and insisted we join them for lunch. One of the men unrolled a mat on the ground and set down a large communal plate, inviting Rob to sit cross-legged beside them. Unsure whether to join them, I waited at a distance from the group. When the men saw this they beckoned me over. I was touched by their hospitality.

One of the men showed us how to take the food with our right hand and roll it into a ball to eat. Rob managed to get some of the rice to his mouth, but I felt like a child who hadn't learned to eat properly and, to my embarrassment, ended up with grains of rice and bits of fish all over my hand and knees. I was grateful when Abdullah explained that we used knives and forks in our country and didn't know how to eat with our hands. The men expressed regret that they didn't have a fork to give me. One of them turned to Rob and asked, "Americans?"

"No, New Zealanders."

Abdullah explained that New Zealand was near Australia.

Another man said he had four wives and twelve children and they all lived harmoniously together in the same house. Through Abdullah, he asked Rob how many wives men could have in New Zealand.

"One. And that's more than enough for harmony," Rob replied.

When Abdullah translated this the men slapped their sides and laughed. They wound a turban around Rob's head which set the whole group off laughing again.

When they finished their meal, one of the men took off his turban and spread it on the ground as his prayer mat. Apart from Abdullah, who wore the traditional long white *dishdasha*, the men all wore a wrap-around piece of cloth covering their legs from the waist down, Yemeni-style. In ancient times there were no borders between the Yemen, Africa and Oman, and in the Dhofar region the Yemeni style was still evident in the way of dress and in the rectangular, high-windowed, mud-brick houses. As we left we thanked the group and promised to send the photos we'd taken of them to Abdullah.

Our next destination was Kawr Rori, a natural harbour on the coast where there was an archaeological dig going on in nearby Sumharum. The excavations had uncovered the ruins of a palace, thought to have been built by the

Queen of Sheba who lived in the Yemen and came to Sumharum for the frankincense trade. The ruins were fenced off and the elderly guard said we weren't allowed in. However, Abdullah managed to wangle the key out of him and led us around the ruins, pointing out the different rooms and the store for the frankincense. He found a tiny piece on the ground and gave it to me. "Maybe the Queen of Sheba held this very piece."

Here, five thousand years ago, frankincense was loaded onto boats in the harbour where now camels were swimming and hundreds of flamingos were resting in the inlet. I wondered if the Queen of Sheba had set out from here on her visit to King Solomon in Jerusalem with her gifts of frankincense, *coming up from the desert like a column of smoke, breathing of myrrh and frankincense.*

Our next stop was Job's Tomb. A simple white building, with a gold-painted dome, it was forty kilometres from Salalah on Jabal Lyttin at the end of a road lined with crimson flame trees, almond, jasmine and pink bougainvillea. At the entrance to the building, an enormous footprint, reputed to be Job's, was encased in stone.

"Job was a giant," said Abdullah. "But as excavation of the tomb is forbidden no one has been able to verify it."

An old grey-bearded man handed me a green headscarf and gestured to us to take off our shoes. As we dropped pieces of frankincense into the burners around the green-cloth-covered tomb and watched the thin spirals of smoke waft up to the ceiling, Abdullah said, "The smoke of frankincense is sacred. It carries our prayers to Heaven."

Rob said, "My mother used to say she needed the patience of Job when I was a child. I never actually knew who Job was and why he needed patience."

"He was a prosperous man with ten healthy children and devoted to God," Abdullah said. "Even when he lost all his wealth and all his children died he still kept his faith without complaining. Then all his friends told him that God does these things for a reason, so Job must have been really bad to have been punished so much. Job asked God to tell him what he had done wrong. God replied that the universe was beautiful and unknowable and that God was not answerable to man."

"Meaning?"

Abdullah shrugged. "Just what it says."

Next day we began our trip into the Empty Quarter, at 5.00am, to avoid the worst of the heat in one of the most arid, dry, and blisteringly hot deserts in the world. The mist of the coming monsoon obscured the skyline and the vast featureless expanses of empty grey sand. For one hundred kilometres we followed the route the explorer, Wilfred Thesiger, took in the 1940s with his Bedouin companions. It was the route taken centuries ago by the camel caravans of the frankincense trade. The Duru tribe of Bedouin still lived there. In times past, Abdullah told us, they used the stars to guide them at night, and the direction of the wind in the daytime. Water was so scarce they drank it only every three or four days. "Nowadays," he said, "water tankers bring them fresh supplies every week."

We stopped near a small stone house occupied by a solitary Bedouin named Mohammed. A few camels were tethered nearby in a barbed-wire enclosure. After greetings and exchanging the 'news', Abdullah asked him if he would give us some camel's milk. Mohammed took a basin over to the enclosure and tied a protesting camel to a stick, then took off the bag that covered her udder to stop her baby suckling. As soon as the baby saw him removing the bag it sprinted over and hung onto one teat while Mohammed grabbed another. All the while mama complained loudly, and this set off a responding roar from a huge black male camel standing inside a separate enclosure. As I wondered how easy it would be for the roaring male to break out of his restraint, Mohammed handed me the basin full of warm, frothy milk. Reminding myself that Thesiger survived for months on camel's milk and dates, I sipped it. It tasted like sweet cow's milk. Abdullah explained cheerfully that I could expect stomach troubles.

Mohammed invited us into his little house, furnished with a bed and some pans on a small stove. He wouldn't allow me to take his photo as he wasn't dressed properly. Through Abdullah I asked him if he rode the camels. "No," he replied, "I sell them in the market for meat."

I asked if he ever got lonely. Shaking his head he proudly showed us his new mobile phone. He stood at the door waving goodbye until we drove out of sight.

We passed a truckload of camels going to market. "We regard them the way you regard cows," Abdullah said.

Our final stop was Shisr, the lost city of Ubar. I told Abdullah that when I was a child I had read a story about this city in *The Arabian Nights*. He said it was also mentioned in 200 AD by Arabian geographers and was marked on a map drawn by Ptolemy. "It was a rich market town at the crossroads of the frankincense trade. The Koran tells us that God punished the inhabitants of Ubar for their sinful ways by destroying the city and making it vanish into the earth."

Several western explorers, including Thesiger, had failed to find the city, until in 1990 American satellite pictures taken over the desert showed traces of ancient caravan routes converging on the area. These pictures, together with help from local Bedouins, enabled a team of archaeologists to locate the ruins. Their excavations revealed an underground stream that had gradually eroded the limestone under the city, causing it to collapse, and creating a huge sinkhole into which most of the city had fallen. The desert eventually crept over the once fertile land and the winds covered it with sand. Now, all that remained above ground were a few stones from the towers that had once stored the frankincense before it was transported across the desert by camel trains.

The museum next to the ruins was closed. However, Abdullah found the man with the keys and persuaded him to open up the museum. His name was Mabruk and he had lived in the area all his life. He spoke good English and described how, as a child, he had listened to his grandfather's stories of a fabled city that had disappeared overnight because of God's anger at the profligate lifestyle of the inhabitants. When the American archaeologists arrived and started excavating, the locals were very excited, he said, and helped them. He showed us photographs of the dig and told stories of the archaeologists. I asked him if he had any conflict in reconciling the archaeological evidence of the slow erosion of the limestone with the traditional belief of God's wrath destroying the city overnight.

"Not at all," he replied. "The Koran is God's word, so there can be no conflict."

Mabruk told us that the frankincense trade, which had once brought enormous wealth to southern Arabia, died with the rise of Christianity. Christians were urged to bury their dead therefore the vast quantities of frankincense previously used at cremations were no longer needed. The economy remained at subsistence level for many centuries until the discovery of oil in the 1960s brought a new cycle of prosperity. Schools, hospitals, and proper housing sprang up on the edge of the desert. Pick-up trucks and four-wheel-drives replaced the camel.

"What frankincense was to ancient times, oil is today," said Abdullah.

We thanked Mabruk and said goodbye. On our way back to the Land Cruiser a group of little boys in white dishdashas and embroidered caps followed us, laughing and chattering. They stood waving as we drove away.

On the motorway back to Salalah there were dozens of migrant Indian workers sweltering in the heat, sweeping sand from the road to keep the ever-encroaching desert at bay. I thought of the civilisations that had risen and fallen there over the millennia, all traces erased by the desert sands. I started saying this to Abdullah when he suddenly swerved around a camel lying in the middle of the motorway. We gasped and held on to our seats.

Abdullah grinned and said, "At the end of life there is only the sound of the desert wind and the tinkling of the camel's bell. That's what the Bedouins say."

Disconnecting

It had taken many frustrating months to get our lives working properly in Oman, but I had no regrets about staying there. The year had fulfilled its purpose. Rob was less sanguine and was looking forward to pulling the plug. However, the process of doing this was no less fraught than the initial plugging-in had been.

First, we went to the insurance office to transfer the insurance of our car to Dom and Marty, who were buying it. Then we drove to the Police Station to complete the transfer of ownership. On the way, I commented that I was amazed we had not had a car accident. We had never become used to seeing mangled cars on the sides of the roads and the occasional dead body. An ambulance service had been launched that year and the ambulances were stationed at various trouble spots. However, as the hard shoulders were often clogged with speeding drivers, the ambulances couldn't always get to the scene of an accident in time.

We were discussing this when a Land Cruiser came charging around the roundabout into the side of our car. We tumbled out, speechless. The Emiratis in the Landcruiser shook our hands then called the Police. At the

Police Station the policemen, who spoke no English, wrote out the report based on what the Emiratis told them and indicated the accident was our fault. The Emiratis said we had to pay them some money or they would take us to court. At that point I called Hafiz and in half an hour he arrived. He asked the Emiratis why they wanted money from us when we already had comprehensive insurance. They looked surprised and said the Police hadn't told them. They shook hands again and left. The policeman told us to come back tomorrow to collect the report for the insurance company.

Next day we trooped back to the Police Station. No one had written the report. The policeman at the desk told us to come back the next day. As we were leaving, a Police Inspector followed us down the steps and heard Rob fuming. He excused himself for interrupting, said he spoke English and asked if we needed help. When we explained what had happened, he rolled his eyes. "The driver of the Land Cruiser is to blame," he said. "He was going too fast. He will be fined." He asked us to go back into the station with him where he would write out the report himself. He signed it and handed it to us, apologising for the 'misunderstanding'. We thanked him for his kindness, hardly able to believe that luck was on our side for once.

With just two weeks left I still didn't know whether the company would refund my airfare home. On the day of my students' graduation, Hussein, with his hand over his heart, made an emotional speech about what a great teacher I was. The students clapped and presented me with gifts: a beautiful wooden box engraved with my name and the dates of the course, containing a silver and amber Bedouin necklace and a piece of weaving. Amina gave me a little box with a gold emblem of Oman. In tears, she asked if she could kiss me. As the other women came up to kiss me the male students stood discreetly at the back of the room. They stayed there while I went outside to be photographed with the women. As we arranged ourselves in front of the school Amina put her mask back over her face and apologised that she could not join us in the photographs. "But I will send you a photo of my son," she whispered.

As the men came out to be photographed with me, Nagwa, Hussein's assistant who was taking the photographs, told me to wait behind after the men returned to the library.

"Take my advice," she whispered. "Do not leave until they pay you, or you won't see a cent."

I stared at her.

She glanced at the door. "I heard Hussein on the phone talking to Mahmoud. He has a letter for you. I think he'll give it to you before he leaves for Egypt. I dare not say more."

Next morning Philippe gave me Hussein's letter. But by then Hussein had scarpered. The letter stated the company would pay my final month's salary, holiday pay and gratuity, but not refund my airfare as "it is company policy to only give tickets."

Philippe averted his eyes. "I've done the best I could," he muttered. "I did tell you to accept the sheik's offer of a 50% discount on the ticket."

It was time to end this issue. I remembered Debbie, the teacher who, a year earlier, had discovered the day before she left Oman that her six months' overtime pay was not included in her final payment. I now recalled the memory of this woman frothing at the mouth with impotent rage. I rang Mahmoud and asked him to pay my final salary a week before I left.

"Of course, Mrs Alexa. No problem."

Kass rolled her eyes. "Don't believe him."

On the day the payment was due, Philippe stuck his head around the door of my office as I was packing up files and teaching notes. He said Mahmoud had just been on the phone to say he didn't have any cheques signed by the sheik. Mahmoud had also pointed out, Philippe said, that although my course with the Ministry of Higher Education was finished and my students had gone, I was still officially under contract, so I needed to do more teaching and Mahmoud had suggested I take over the evening classes. What did I think?

What I thought was to stuff Philippe in my car and drive with him and Kass across town to Head Office, ignoring Philippe's protests that while he could understand I was upset, he was sure his own presence was not really required and that this situation could have been averted had I accepted the Sheik's generous offer of 50% of the return airfare in the first place. No doubt Kass had influenced me to hold out for more, he said, ignoring Kass's glare, but I must surely realise all this confrontation would get me nowhere. Had my year in the Gulf taught me nothing? And in the event of a meltdown at Head Office, he, Philippe, could not intervene. After all, he still had to work here and these guys could make his life unbearable and after all it was only money.

Mahmoud was sitting in his chair behind his desk with a smile pasted on his face. He produced the book of blank cheques and smiled again. He would send a driver to the town where the sheik was staying and get him to sign a cheque and then the driver would return. The cheque might be in my account on Thursday. Or Saturday. Or Sunday. Anyway, sometime soon. *Inshallah.*

"So why can't you just give it to me in cash?"

"Unfortunately, I do not have the cash."

"You're telling me that despite this company owning hotels and travel agencies, you don't have enough cash to pay me?"

"That's correct."

"In that case," I said, "Rob will fly to Brazil alone for our friend's wedding and I will stay in Oman by myself until all the money is in the bank. Until it is, I will withhold my end-of-course reports for the Ministry of Higher Education and I'll need to send an e-mail to every student and the Ministry to explain why."

Mahmoud's smile frayed around the edges as he weighed up the odds that I was bluffing. Philippe's sharp intake of breath convinced him otherwise. With his smirk now a straight line he opened a drawer and pulled out some cash. Then he picked up the phone and asked for the balance to be brought over that evening.

"It will be in your account in the morning."

"Good."

He could barely contain his annoyance. "When you leave Oman the Public Relations Officer must accompany you to the airport to cancel your visa. You must give him your Labour Card."

"Of course."

"And your Alcohol Licence."

"Naturally."

"And you will need to teach evening classes next week."

"No problem."

"And Ahmed will need to inspect your flat.'

"Because …"

"Because you might have broken something." His composure was returning. "When are you leaving? In a week, you said?"

"I'll check the date and time of the flight and let you know."

Next morning, ten minutes before the bank was due to close for the weekend, I watched Mahmoud hand over the cash, minus my return airfare, to the teller. Then I transferred the money to New Zealand while he looked on. Before he left he said, "Ahmed will be doing his inspection after the weekend, so make sure you leave the flat clean."

"Absolutely," I smiled.

We went back to the flat and packed our cases. Early next morning Kass, Dom and Marty took us to the airport. Before we boarded I said to them, "You showed me how to laugh again. I'll always be grateful to you for that."

Kass hugged me. "I'll be leaving this place soon. I'll find myself a place in the world with four seasons and things to look forward to."

"Forget all this crap," said Dom.

"But don't forget us," said Marty. "And all our good times."

The lights of Dubai looked like thousands of pinheads below. We unbuckled our seat belts, accepted a glass of water from the flight attendant and let out a long sigh of relief.

"What do you think will piss him off most?" Rob asked. "The fact you escaped his greedy little paws, or that you escaped with your Labour Card and your Alcohol Licence?"

"Kass'll be our fly-on-the-wall," I said. "I only hope the little toad doesn't take it out on her."

"She'll handle him," said Rob. "Thank God we're outta there."

"Yes. But still ..." I looked at the pattern of tiny red leaves and flowers curling around my fingers, hands and wrists.

Aisha: "*We made the henna ourselves. From a shrub I have in my garden.*"

Thuraya: "*We ground the leaves.*"

Fayza: "*And mixed them with water, lemon juice and rose oil.*"

Amal: "*Each flower is a signature from all of us.*"

Fatma: "*It won't wash off. The design will only fade as new skin cells replace your old ones.*"

Noora: "*So you will never forget us.*"

Amina: "*As we will never forget you.*"

Between streaks of cloud I glimpsed miles and miles and miles of desert. I thought about Kass telling me how she'd stopped by an aviation club one day during a bleak period in her life and asked to be taken up in a glider. She'd said, "I just wanted to be flown around the sun and silence and watch the world from above."

I'd told her about the time my son-in-law, to celebrate getting his pilot's license, flew us from Christchurch to Kaikoura in a four-seater Cherokee Warrior. As we flew over the Canterbury Plains we could see our house below. To allow us to see it more closely he did a maximum rating turn which defied gravity. I didn't know where the horizon was or where 'up' and 'down' were. As he pulled out of the turn I was frozen, disorientated, dislocated. When my breathing returned to normal I decided to get a bus back to Christchurch when we landed in Kaikoura. But the sky was so blue and the sea sparkled with light and I was fascinated by the way the plains connected to the mountains, the rivers flowed to the sea and the forests turned into scrub. "It was such a powerful metaphor that by the time we got to Kaikoura the idea of travelling back by bus evaporated," I said.

Kass blew a smoke ring in the air. She watched it slowly disintegrate.

Brazil

2004

Shadows

Bill and Rosy's house was full of ghosts. Rosy's spinning wheel sat in the same corner in the same place. Bill's books still littered the table in his library. The puppy, Augustinha, creaked up the steps on her ten-year-old legs, accompanied by a puppy of her own. Rosy shooed them into the kitchen then brought out dessert. Sally still looked sixteen, but the previous week she'd had her twenty-fifth birthday. She told us she was leaving for the USA at the end of the month to do her Masters degree. Outside their guest house in the garden, where we were staying, was the barbecue where we'd all gathered on our last day in Brazil nine years ago. Sally saw me looking at it though the window and said, "Do you know we've sold the farm?"

"What!"

"It was getting harder and harder to keep it going," said Bill. "Every time we went back something else had gotten stolen. Then the farmer next door started a factory melting down lead batteries! The smell and the noise just wrecked the place. He'd built it right by the lake where we used to swim and read and chill out. It wasn't the same place anymore."

When I finally found my voice I said, "I can't imagine you selling it. I thought it was so much a part of you that you would keep it forever."

Rosy and Sally glanced at each other. Sally said, "They sold it when I was in the States. I couldn't believe it! All the horses gone."

No one spoke for a minute then Bill said, "Beth's painting of the horse that I hung up in the little library was stolen. The trail that she helped us make through the bush is still there. I guess you'll want to walk through there?"

We nodded.

After lunch they took us to see the new language school which they'd bought and renovated with the proceeds from the farm sale. They showed us photographs of a run-down building surrounded by other buildings in the same state. It was hard to believe the house was the same one we were admiring now in its little garden full of flowers and trees.

"Every time we worked in the garden and planted something new someone would stop by and ask us the name of the plant," said Rosy. "We started to notice the other houses on the street were being bought and painted. That one over there is a boutique. The one over the road is a café."

"And they've all got gardens," added Bill. "That's something you rarely see here."

I turned and looked down the street full of people and saw our old Portuguese teacher Sebastiana. We both stared at each other in disbelief. She ran across the street calling,

"*Meu Deus! Nao accredito!*" Her eyes were full of tears. She flung her arms around me and then Rob and in halting English told us how sad she was about Beth. "I pray for her every day, Alexa. I think of you all the time." She invited us to her house on Thursday morning. More ghosts, but I was moved by her tears.

In the afternoon Sally took us to the farm. Bill said he hadn't been back since he sold it. He didn't want to see the changes.

As we turned in at the gate I thought of the newspaper clippings they had sent us over the years, all the updates on the new buildings and the development of the riding school. "It was Dad's dream," said Sally, "and he sold it!"

"We can't live in the past, Sal," said Rob. "It's good your folks have moved on."

We pulled up by the old barn. The roof over the horse stalls had fallen in and scattered over the ground. An old saddle lay on a beam, covered in bird droppings. We walked along the track to the house that Bill had built many years ago, where Beth had been impressed to find a black hairy spider as big as her hand, past the empty chicken house, past the lake, past the place I'd taken a photo of Beth riding Cristiane with the foal Beija Flor trotting alongside and the three geese in a line behind.

"She never walked anywhere, did she?" Sally said. "She always ran. And jumped over gates. That's what I remember most. And the number of times she got thrown off the horses and got straight back on." She laughed then looked at me. "You never knew about the falls, did you?"

I shook my head.

The old wooden house had gone. The saddling, the grooming, the picnics, the singing, the laughter, all gone. A new house was being erected on the site of the old one.

"Oh no ..." Sally whispered. "If Dad saw this ..."

But the lake was still the same. I left Sally and Rob by the edge of the water, crossed the bridge and walked around to the other side. The pain in my throat spread to my chest.

In the evening Bill took us to see Simone's house. He'd called the tenant, an artist, to see if we could go. Five years ago, Simone had, by chance, at a conference in Brasilia, met the man who'd been her first boyfriend, Roberto. She married Roberto here in her garden then went to live with him in Washington in the USA. We would travel there to see her, after leaving Brazil.

I looked for the tree outside what had been our bedroom, but the branch that had looked like an impaled woman was no longer there. I looked for the owl, but couldn't see him either. The dogs, the geese, were gone. The garden was the same, but the hammocks on the verandah where Beth had lain reading her books and doing her schoolwork, were gone. The seats where Isadora and Simone had sung their songs were gone. We walked around the rooms. It was a mistake to come here. What was I expecting to find? There was nothing here but shadows.

Bill dropped us off in the centre of town. We passed the apartment building where we had lived in our first weeks in Uberlândia, and the ice cream shop where we had sat every evening to eat ice cream to cool down. The tiny blue church like a music box was still there and all the old buildings. We sat under the *sibiperuna,* a huge ancient tree outside a bar where we used to go with Simone. Just as it started to rain we found we were outside the museum. We had wanted to see it years ago, but it was being renovated then. This time it was full of pictures of the original town.

Later in the afternoon we visited Sebastiana. We laughed and joked about the lessons she'd given us years ago and how Rob had always ended up with a headache. I told her that as we walked along the street to her house today Rob said he felt guilty because he hadn't done his homework. She roared with laughter.

In the evening Rob went out for a meal with Bill and some people from the university and I stayed behind and talked to Rosy. She told me that when they heard about Beth they just couldn't believe it and they had all sat and cried. We talked for a long time and outside the rain poured down in great drops. I told her we were going to Belo Horizonte for Leonardo's wedding.

"How do you feel about that?" she asked.

"I'm glad he's found someone to make him happy," I said.

★

Leonardo was at the airport in Belo Horizonte to meet us. He drove us to his apartment which was crowded with some of his relatives. There, we met Carolina for the first time. She was small with long black hair and seemed nervous around us. Leonardo had met her when he'd gone back to Brazil after Beth had broken up with him and his internship at the hospital in Christchurch had finished. He left Carolina behind when he returned to New Zealand to be with Beth before she died.

Later, we went to his mother's apartment for a meal. Leonardo stayed overnight at his mother's and we returned to his apartment with his cousin, her husband and little girl. Next morning, Francisca, the mother of Agostino, whom I had taught in Christchurch, came to take us to a traditional market. The last time I had seen her was a year and a half ago when she was studying English in Christchurch, too. She was a highly energetic, funny and kind person. She was screaming with laughter as she recalled the time I was driving her to our house and the car ran over some wire which tangled itself around the tyre. She reminded me how we both lay flat under the car on the deserted country road trying to figure out what to do to untangle the wire when a truck roared up and out jumped three young men who sorted the whole thing out for us before charging off into the sunset.

The market was fascinating with all kinds of food, spices, cheeses, baskets, all of which I would have liked to take back to New Zealand, but there wasn't a spare inch in our suitcases. Agostino met us in the market and we had lunch at a restaurant where we also met up with Leonardo. After that Francisca whisked me off to a salon where she'd fixed up an appointment for our hair and nails. Then we had just enough time to head back to the apartment to get changed and go to the church.

We were part of a group of *padrinhos*, (Godparents) and we waited outside the church until Leonardo's mother, Julia, arrived, half an hour late. No one seemed surprised that the wedding started forty-five minutes late. When Julia arrived, Leonardo walked up the aisle with her past the seated five hundred guests. Our *padrinho* group walked up the aisle behind them and sat at the front. The two little flower girls and the page boy walked up next and sat by the altar. Leonardo was standing at the front. The choir that he was a part of sang 'Climb Every Mountain', then he continued the song by himself as Carolina made her entrance in her beautiful white dress with its long train. Leonardo stepped forward to greet her and take her up to the altar.

The service was short. The priest, who was also Carolina's Godfather, was a Dutchman who had lived in Brazil for fifty years. He told everyone that Alexa and Rob, Leonardo's good friends, had come all the way from New Zealand to attend the wedding, then he repeated the same in English and welcomed us "with joy and happiness."

The reception was held on the top floor of a club and there was a live band playing. The volume control on the sound system had broken and the volume was at head-shattering level. It was impossible to hear any conversation, so we moved to the balcony outside. Carolina came out too, with Leonardo behind her. When she saw me there she looked anxious. Without thinking, I raised my hand and lightly touched her face. She smiled.

New Zealand

2004 – 2007

A different road

Our city. Our road. Our house. Our garden. Beth's cats on the front step, disdainful and unforgiving of our desertion. They were round and fat. Melanie had taken good care of them. The dog, disbelieving at first, then all ecstatic legs and tail.

Rob opened our front door and we carried our cases in. Everything looked the same. Melanie had lived here with her children for a whole year. The living room had a different smell. A different kind of energy. I opened the door to Beth's room. Rob followed. The books and pens and oil pastel sketches on her desk were exactly as we had left them a year ago. Her clothes still hung in her cupboard, unused. I touched them with my hand. I held the sleeve of her jacket to see if it still had her smell. It didn't. Her calendar was still on April, the month she had died. Her room was silent. We had been away for a whole year and had returned. But our daughter was still dead.

"She'll always be dead," I said to Rob.

He stood behind me and put his arms around my shoulders. From the window we could see the rowan tree where we had buried Beth's ashes. The tree had reached the top of the fence.

★

Next morning, I opened an email from Kass. My circum-
venting the departure procedure in Oman had resulted in
Kass having to bear the brunt of Hussein's fury. He told
her he would not pay her final month's salary, nor was she
to be allowed to leave the country to go on her planned
holiday to Venice. If she attempted to leave, he threatened,
she would be listed as an absconder and arrested. She went
to the British Embassy which informed him otherwise. She
left the company and the country and flew to a new job in
Greece. Hussein's last act of vengeance was to withhold
her salary until she was at the airline check-in counter.
Dom and Marty were refused the letter of release they
needed to take up a lucrative job with another company in
Oman. They left for Thailand.

The next email was from Philippe, demanding the
immediate return of my Labour Card. The Ministry would
not allow the company to employ another teacher until
the Labour Card was returned. As I read it I thought I'd
like to have been a fly on the wall when Mahmoud,
Hussein and the Sheik received their roasting from the
Ministry. Leaving a week early like that was a breach of
my contract, Philippe fumed. Leaving without telling him
was unprofessional and would make it difficult for him to
convince the company to pay other teachers at the end of
their contracts. I should be mindful of my responsibility to
him, especially considering the amount of time he had
devoted to my contractual issues and nor should I forget

how he had supported me in Mahmoud's office and therefore I owed it to him to contact a courier forthwith and return the Labour Card without further delay.

I pondered on the best response.

Ah yes.

"Leave it with me, Philippe," I wrote. "I'll get back to you."

Then I read Amina's email and wrote a reply. I told her the photo of her baby was beautiful. And yes, I did think he looked like her. And yes, the flower she drew on my wrist was still there, though the henna had started to fade a little. And no, I wouldn't ever forget her. And yes, oh yes, I was happy to be home.

New beginnings

Rob and I waited at the airport in Christchurch watching Leonardo, Carolina and their son, Ferne emerge through the doors. The baby was one year old and they had brought him to New Zealand to introduce him to us. He looked like Leonardo. I wrapped my arms around all three of them.

Rob opened the front door to our house and helped to carry in the cases. Carolina looked around. "Oh, I looking forward so long time to come here. To see and know what Leonardo have seen and know."

As Leonardo brought in the last case, a fantail flew through the door, flew around our heads and perched on a ceiling beam, watching us. Leonardo's eyes filled with tears. Carolina looked at me.

"I think she don't mind I am here, Alexa?"

I touched her arm. "No, she doesn't."

Carolina sat beside Olivia at the table, working on a needle-felted teddy bear that Olivia was teaching her to make. The baby was asleep. Leonardo was sitting in another room at the computer. Carolina was trying to describe her pregnancy.

"I was so shocked – just three weeks after my wedding. I was no prepared for such a thing. I cry and cry. Then my mother she tell me I should talk to my baby in my belly. I talk to him for nine months. But …" she paused, struggling for the words. "I have say this to no one before. Every time I talk to him, it was not to the baby inside my body. It was to a man standing by my side. A much older, wiser man than me."

Olivia stopped sewing and glanced at me.

"I feel so scared for this responsibility. When my baby is born, I can no see him like a baby. I do not want this responsibility. I am so afraid. Then, after fifty days I understand he have chosen me for his mother. He want me to take care him, like a baby, not like a man. So then, I decide to be his mother. He is my baby."

After Leonardo, Carolina and Ferne returned to Brazil our lives filled up again with work, gardening, friends, family. In the middle of all that there was still a great gaping empty space.

On Beth's birthday, we woke to find snow had fallen in the night. We couldn't go to work and the electricity and phone were cut off. Olivia was staying with us. She said remembering Beth on her birthday caused her pain and she needed to be with us this week. She said, "I feel as if I'm crying inside. Nothing is happening on the outside.

The tears are all on the inside. Grieving is like bleeding inside."

I felt her pain in my belly, but I could do nothing to take it away. Sam had left New Zealand to begin a new life in Australia and I was glad he had found a way to deal with his own pain.

In the evening, Olivia persuaded us to go for a walk along the tractor tyre tracks in the snow. We put on coats, hats, scarves and boots, and plodded along the road. The trees and garden and paddocks were blanketed in white. The sun had almost disappeared behind the mountains and the paddocks were soaked in violet light. We passed Vincent's house. It looked like a Victorian English Christmas card with the snow piled high on the sloping roof. Vincent was in hospital again. His lung cancer had progressed to the point that it was unlikely he'd come out this time. I thought of all his irises and daffodils under the snow, all the bulbs he'd planted.

When we returned from Oman I asked Melanie to help me re-train Jack before I sold him. I didn't know then that Vincent was back in the picture. I didn't know he'd never really left the picture. I didn't know about his threats to Melanie over helping me with the horse until her agoraphobia prevented her from leaving her house.

We reached the top of the road and turned the corner to see a huge yellow moon hanging in the indigo sky. Olivia took photographs. "Oh Mum," she breathed, "We might never see such a sight again. It's so beautiful it makes you want to cry."

We turned to walk back home. The road looked different in the snow. The night was drawing in. I thought of the candles we would light and the blazing log fire we would sit by. I thought of the books we would read and the cats who would sit on our laps. I was walking between Rob and Olivia and I was glad we were together to share this night and the moon and the snow.

Acknowledgements

Thank you to the editors of the following publications in which different versions of these stories have appeared.

- *Connotation Press* – The bough breaks; I'll get back to you;
- *Corpus Journal of Medical Humanities, University of Otago* – The stone;
- *Fictive Dream* – The man in the moon; The colour of sunshine; The desert wind and the tinkling of the camel's bell;
- *National Flash Fiction Day Anthology 'Sleep is a Beautiful Colour'* – The quick and the dead;
- *Peacock Journal* – Bridging the gap;
- *Retreat West Books Soul Etchings* – Grit;
- *Takahē* – The season for burning;
- *The Blue Nib* – Dawn trek in the Wahiba Desert; The skin that separates water and air; The night of the goddess;
- *The International Literary Quarterly* – When the wind died;
- *The Story Shack* – Kassidy's roof;
- *Words for the Wild* – Just an old grey Volkswagen;
- *X-Ray Literary Magazine* – Pablo's hair.

Thanks

My heartfelt thanks to publisher Matt Potter for his editing advice and his belief in my work.

Also from Truth Serum Press

truthserumpress.net/catalogue/

- *Love, Lemons and Illicit Sex* by Nod Ghosh
  978-1-923000-06-3 (paperback) 978-1-923000-09-4 (ePub)
- *Hold Off the Night* by Teresa Burns Gunther
  978-1-922427-00-7 (paperback) 978-1-922427-18-2 (ePub)
- *Remembering the Dead* by Lewis Woolston
  978-1-922427-58-8 (paperback) 978-1-922427-62-5 (ePub)

- *How to Catch Flathead* by Peter Michal
  978-1-925536-94-2 (paperback) 978-1-925536-95-9 (ePub)
- *Easy Money* by Steve Evans
  978-1-925536-81-2 (paperback) 978-1-925536-82-9 (ePub)
- *The Last Free Man* by Lewis Woolston
  978-1-925536-88-1 (paperback) 978-1-925536-89-8 (ePub)